DEATH IN A FAMILY WAY

Gwendolyn Southin

Copyright © 2008 Gwendolyn Southin

All rights reserved. No part of this publication may be reproduced, stored in a retrieval system, or transmitted in any form or by any means—electronic, mechanical, audio recording, or otherwise—without the written permission of the publisher or a photocopying licence from Access Copyright, Toronto, Canada.

TouchWood Editions
#108 –17665 66A Avenue
Surrey, BC V3S 2A7
www.touchwoodeditions.com

TouchWood Editions
PO Box 468
Custer, WA
98240-0468

Library and Archives Canada Cataloguing in Publication
Southin, Gwendolyn
Death in a family way / Gwendolyn Southin.

ISBN 978-1-894898-72-0

I. Title.

PS8587.O978D42 2008   C813'.6   C2008-900300-4

Library of Congress Control Number: 2008921287

Proofread by Christine Savage
Book design by R-House Design
Cover image and design by Tobyn Manthorpe

Printed in Canada

TouchWood Editions acknowledges the financial support for its publishing program from the Government of Canada through the Book Publishing Industry Development Program (BPIDP), Canada Council for the Arts, and the province of British Columbia through the British Columbia Arts Council and the Book Publishing Tax Credit.

This book has been produced on 100% post-consumer recycled paper, processed chlorine free and printed with vegetable-based dyes.

To Vic for your support and to my writers group—
The Quintessential Writers—Betty Keller, Rosella Leslie,
Maureen Foss and Dorothy Fraser for your help and
encouragement.

PROLOGUE

Seagull crested the wave, heeled over, and slid into the darkness of the next trough. The sea cascaded over the thin canvas cover protecting the controls and the two front seats. "I can't swim," Larry heard the girl scream above the howling gale. "Let's go back!"

Larry ignored her as he wrenched desperately on the wheel, trying to bring the boat head-on again before the next wave struck. This time, Seagull's wooden hull shuddered and creaked as she slewed broadside, and the girl screamed again, bracing herself against the forward bulwark as water sloshed over the gunwales.

"Go back," the girl pleaded. "Please go back!"

Larry's response as the boat wallowed in the next trough was to give the girl a vicious backhander across the face. "Stop screaming, you stupid bitch," he snarled.

She slumped into the seat again, covering her face with her hands. "Are we go . . . going . . . to . . . to drown?" she whimpered.

Larry didn't even glance at her. "Put your bloody life jacket on and start bailing."

At that moment, the moon, peeping through the scudding clouds just above the horizon, outlined the distant coastline of Washington State, and Larry, switching off Seagull's running lights, headed her toward land.

Beside him, the girl, struggling to zip up her life jacket, yelled,

"Look! A light!" And she stood, holding her swollen stomach with both hands, as if to protect the growing baby inside her.

"Point Roberts," he shouted back.

"No," the girl said. "No, it's coming toward us!"

As the approaching launch cut through the waves, its searchlight scanned the black, froth-capped water. Larry, letting out a stream of obscenities, wrenched the wheel hard over just as the beam bathed *Seagull* in light.

"What are you doing?" the girl cried. "They can help us."

"Don't be stupid!"

"This is the US Coast Guard," a voice boomed through the darkness. "What craft are you?"

Larry's answer was to push *Seagull*'s powerful motor to its limit as he swung her away from the Coast Guard cutter and headed back toward the Canadian border.

"Heave to or we'll shoot," the voice boomed again as the searchlight caught *Seagull* in its glare. A moment later, the first shot skimmed over their heads.

"Keep down," Larry screamed at the girl.

Then, as the boat rose on a towering swell, a second shot found its mark on *Seagull*, shattering the windshield. A third shot hit the hull with a sickening thud, and the boat bucketed from side to side. The girl, glancing back, saw with horror that her canvas holdall, stowed in the aft cockpit, was floating in ankle-deep water. "Oh my God," she moaned. "We're going to die."

The moon sank into the sea, and in the pre-dawn darkness, Larry could no longer tell what direction he was going. He only knew that the Coast Guard seemed to have given up the chase. "Must be over the border," he told himself.

An hour passed as Larry clung to the wheel of the foundering boat, listening to the ever-increasing wind and praying the motor wouldn't quit. Beside him, the girl sobbed quietly as *Seagull* settled lower in the water. Then, in the first flush of dawn light as the storm winds began to die, he caught a glimpse of land. "Gulf Islands," he muttered.

"What?" the girl said.

Larry had completely forgotten her. "Gulf Islands," he said again, abruptly altering course toward the islands.

"Oh God! We'll be saved now, won't we?" And she stood just as a wave broadsided *Seagull*. This time, despite Larry's efforts to right her, the boat heeled over, and the next wave swept the girl overboard into the black foaming sea.

As the cold water closed over her, she thought she heard her baby cry—but it was only the screech of gulls wheeling overhead, searching for the storm's debris in the dawn light.

CHAPTER ONE

Margaret Spencer put down her coffee cup and opened the large white envelope that was lying beside her plate. She pulled out a glossy birthday card decorated with a bouquet of violets and anemones. As she opened the card, a twenty-dollar bill fell out; absently, she picked it up while reading the verse printed inside:

> To my wife so thoughtful and sweet,
> The girl I was lucky to meet,
> By my side thru' the years ...

She shuddered and skipped the rest of the verse to read the bottom of the card:

> To Margaret,
> Fondest Love, Harry.

I wonder who picked that lulu out. I can hear him saying to his secretary, "Get something with flowers and a suitable verse." Then she scolded herself, *That's being unkind. He probably bought it himself on his lunch hour.*

She stared at the dateline on the top of the newspaper Harry held in front of his face. She had actually forgotten that today was her birthday, but there it was on the paper: March 20, 1958. She really was fifty years old. Harry lowered the paper to look at her. Marmalade quivered on one end of his ginger moustache. "Thought you'd rather have the money and buy something yourself. Never know what to get you." He paused. "I'll have another cup of coffee."

Margaret put down the card, picked up the coffee pot and, leaning forward, filled his cup. She spread marmalade on a piece of toast and bit into it. Across the table, her husband of twenty-eight years finished his coffee and wiped his mouth fastidiously on his serviette. She hoped he would miss the marmalade on his moustache, but with a final flourish, he wiped it off. He stood, carefully refolded the newspaper and placed it beside Margaret, then bent down to peck her lightly on the cheek. "Happy birthday."

Rising from the table, she followed Harry into the hall, picking up his brown leather briefcase from the oak chair as she passed. She carried it to the front door, where she waited while he struggled into his overcoat, put his hat on his head and held out his hand for the case. "I've a four o'clock meeting with Harris today," he said, as he opened the door. "And you know what he's like. I'll probably be late." He paused while he sniffed the outside air. "I think I'll take my umbrella, Margaret." He waited while she got it from the hallstand. "As I was saying," he continued, taking the furled umbrella from her, "if you want to celebrate your birthday, it'll have to be Saturday."

She watched him back his brand new, dark blue Chrysler Windsor out of the drive and, as usual, lift his hand to wave as he passed the house. The draft from the car picked up last year's brown and yellow leaves and swirled them in circles. Once the leaves were airborne, the wind carried them even higher before abruptly dropping them to the ground.

She gave a shiver, closed the door and walked back into the kitchen. She picked the card up and read the verse right through this time. *My God! Fifty!* She had to fight the feeling of panic that suddenly engulfed her. *What have I got to show for my life?*

She cleared the table and carried the dishes to the sink, where she carefully washed and dried them before putting them away. Climbing the stairs, she looked at their double bed from the doorway. *What happened to us?* she wondered as she walked into the room and began to pull the sheets straight. *When did we grow apart?* She had met Harry in England in the spring of 1929. He was on a visit to some aged aunts on his mother's side. Margaret, who had just started work as a clerk-typist in the local solicitor's office in Maidstone, Kent, had thought how handsome and sophisticated he was. To her parents' dismay, the courtship had been brief, and within four months she was leaving England to come to Vancouver with him. The Wall Street Crash came less than a month later, and Harry's small corporate law practice dwindled immediately. At first he had been adamant that his wife was not going to work outside their home, but when he had to let his secretary go, he had welcomed all the help she could give him. She remembered the excitement of those early years, working beside him in the office, but after struggling to build up his clientele for another four years, Harry had admitted defeat. Margaret discovering that she was pregnant clinched the matter, and he agreed to accept a junior role in his father's established firm. *I guess it was the years of bringing up the two girls that pushed us apart. We were both too busy—he trying to impress his father and I trying to be the perfect mother. I was always tired, and Harry had such a hard time understanding small children.* She gave the eiderdown a hard yank and then sat down heavily on her side of the bed. *But*, she thought as she smoothed the silky texture of the bedspread, *he was never really interested in the girls, even when they got older.*

She stood up and walked over to look at herself in the full-length mirror on the closet door. *Not bad for fifty. Could lose a few pounds.* She reached for her hairbrush from the dressing table. "There's nothing wrong with you, old girl," she told herself sternly as she brushed her still-brown, curly hair. "Just pull yourself together and go and spend Harry's twenty dollars on something totally extravagant."

A short time later, still dressed in her housecoat, she sat at the kitchen table with Harry's discarded newspaper. *Perhaps there's a sale at the Bay.*

As usual, Thursday's paper was extra thick. The front page headline, bold and black, jumped out at her: POLICE TRAP SUSPECT BY POSING AS DOCTORS. She started to scan the article, but she wasn't really in the mood for crime, so she skipped the pages until she came to the insert that featured the latest fashions. The Hudson's Bay department store ads were completely devoted to trousseau stuff for the spring bride. Woodwards, its competitor, not to be outdone, had taken a whole page to show men's formal attire; several other store ads were for baby and infant clothes. *Nothing exciting there for me.* She bypassed the general news and the women's section that featured hamburger served in a dozen different ways, then came to the classifieds. She ran her eyes down the columns of the Help Wanted—Female section. "Let's see, just for fun: private secretary, photo shop assistant. Here's a good one... Top-Notch Manager for Ultra-Modern Shirt Laundry." She started to giggle. "I can just see Harry's face at me leaving for work in the morning with my iron in hand." She reached the end of the column and was starting on the next when a small ad in bold type fairly jumped out at her. *Mature woman for small office, experience not necessary, some typing, answer telephone, hours nine to one.* The telephone number followed.

Well, I can imagine that one's been snapped up. She continued reading, but found herself returning to the ad again and again.

Carrying the newspaper over to the telephone, she picked up the receiver, then replaced it on its cradle. "This is silly," she said, resolutely picking it up again. "If it's busy, it's an omen." She dialed the number.

"SO WHEN ARE YOU going to get some help around here?" Sergeant Sawasky asked. He settled himself into the chair across the desk from his former partner, Nat Southby. "You sure could do with some," he added, looking disparagingly at the litter of paper on the desk and piled in boxes on the floor. "This office is an unholy mess!"

"I've had an ad running in the paper for the past week," Nat answered. "But so far all I've gotten have been duds."

"You're just too damn picky," George said with a laugh. "Bet you're looking for a sweater girl. A hard-boiled blonde with big bazooms."

Nat leaned back into his swivel armchair and puffed on his foul-smelling cigar. "I'll tell you this much, George, I would settle for some nice, middle-aged woman if she was able to type without making too many mistakes and could make some kind of order out of this mess."

"Well, how's business anyway?"

"Picking up. Couldn't be any worse than last year, for Pete's sake," Nat answered, tapping the ash off his cigar. "And the cases are getting more interesting. Not so many deadbeats and missing husbands."

"It must be nearly four years since you quit the force."

"Would you believe six last month?"

"Well, we still miss you at the precinct, but you were wise in leaving when you did. That Mulligan affair sure tainted the force."

"Yeah? I'm no saint, George, but I draw the line at all that graft and greed. Hell," he continued savagely, "I thought I was in the force to protect people, not turn a blind eye while the chief of police is lining his pockets." He paused and took a drag at his cigar. "We were all taken in by Mulligan. All of us." He leaned back into his chair, his thoughts returning to the days when he had been a rookie on the vice squad. "He was going to clean up the city, remember? What a joke!" He took another drag at his cigar. "I thought he was for real, you know, but being on vice I found out what was really happening. Even though I managed to get a transfer to homicide, the force had lost its appeal. Maybe I was too much of an idealist. I admire you, though, for sticking with it."

"Yeah? Well I admire your guts for getting out. But it's different for me. I've a wife and kids depending on me. I can't afford the luxury of idealism." George got up from his chair. "Things are a lot better under George Archer, you know, but I still miss your ugly face." He smiled as he reached up and took his coat down from the bamboo coat tree. "But that guy Farthing they moved into your spot is one goddam pain in the ass." He gave a huge sigh. "Ah well, see you around," he said as he opened the outside door. "And I expect to see that beautiful blonde sitting at the front desk the next time I come."

The phone gave a shrill ring.

"There's your blonde," Sawasky grinned as he went out.

"No such luck," Nat answered as he reached for the instrument. "Hello."

"Oh . . . excuse me. Is it . . . ? It's about your ad . . . in the paper?" Margaret suddenly felt very foolish. "I expect it's taken," she finished lamely.

"No, as a matter of fact, it isn't, not yet," Nat replied, reaching for a notepad. "How'd you like to give me some particulars? Starting with your name."

"My name . . . oh, my name is Margaret . . . Margaret Spencer, and your ad did say 'experience not necessary,' and I'm afraid that's it. I've very little."

Nat laughed and Margaret liked the sound of it. An open, confident laugh, she thought.

"That's okay, then," he said, "but do you fill the other requirement—mature person?"

Margaret found herself laughing too. "Oh yes, that one I do fill," she answered, looking directly over at Harry's birthday card propped on the mantelpiece.

"Could you come down to the office for an interview—say this afternoon around two o'clock?"

"This afternoon? I guess so," she replied slowly.

"Where do you live, Mrs. Spencer?"

"Kerrisdale. On Elm."

"That's perfect," he answered. "My office is 1687 West Broadway, Suite 301. Do you know the area? It's between Fir and Pine. It'll take you about twenty minutes or so by bus."

"Yes," Margaret answered slowly. I know the district quite well. Whom do I ask for?"

"The name's Nat. Nat Southby. It's on the door."

"All right, Mr. Southby. I'll see you at two, then." She replaced the receiver and sat down with a thump on the chair next to the telephone table, a dazed look on her face.

I didn't ask any of the right questions . . . What kind of business is he in? What salary does it pay? It's absolutely out of the question . . . what will Harry say? I should call him back and say I can't make it. But instead, Margaret went to the hall mirror and looked herself up and down. And, without fully realizing it, she took the first timid step toward changing her life.

CHAPTER TWO

It was close to lunchtime and Broadway was thick with people, buses and parked cars. Margaret soon gave up the attempt to find a parking spot for her small red Morris Minor on the main drag, and instead turned off onto Fir, where, even though the traffic was lighter, she was still lucky to find a place just being vacated.

Most of the buildings in the 1600-block were two and three storeys high, with offices and garment factories on the upper floors and shops at street level. The business of selling spilled out onto the sidewalk: right next door to a second-hand shop where old books and magazines were displayed on a rickety table was a small Italian bakery, and next to that a Chinese grocery with pails of cut flowers, boxes of vegetables and potted plants. As Margaret joined the lunchtime strollers, the smell of freshly baked bread mingled with the rich aroma of ground coffee and made her realize that in her nervousness to be punctual, she'd forgotten to eat lunch.

Halfway down the block, she found number 1687 easily enough and saw that although the brick building was old, it was not quite as rundown as the neighbours that hemmed it in on either side. A photo shop occupied the ground floor, but next to it stood a glass door leading into a kind of small lobby area.

Resolutely, she pushed it open. Immediately in front of her was a narrow staircase, and beside it an old elevator waited for passengers, its sliding steel gate open, all lights off. One look at the elevator convinced her to choose the stairs, but by the time she had climbed the three flights, she wished that she had accepted the dingy elevator's invitation. Puffing with exertion, she walked along the dimly lit corridor to number 301. "Southby's Investigations," she read on the grimy sign. "Please Walk In."

The room she entered overlooked Broadway. She just had time to notice a wooden desk with a Remington typewriter on it, and next to it two battered green filing cabinets, their open drawers spilling out buff folders bulging with photographs and papers, before a man's voice called, "Come in."

Looking around, she realized that the voice was coming from a partly open connecting door. As she pushed gently on it, clouds of cigar smoke wafted out over her head, forming eddies and swirls before slipping through an air vent in the ceiling of the outer office.

Hesitantly poking her head around the door, she saw a rather untidy man sitting behind a desk piled high with more buff folders and papers. He stood up as she entered, immediately tried to hitch up his sagging pants, stubbed a half-smoked cigar into an overflowing ashtray and, with a nod, indicated a chair.

"Sit down, Mrs. . . . uh . . ." He rummaged through the mess on his desk and finally came up with a scrap of paper. "Ah, yes, Mrs. Spencer, isn't it?"

Margaret nodded, at a loss for words.

He brushed cigar ash off his already stained jacket and sat down. For a moment, he just looked at her. The blue of her smart Chanel wool suit matched her eyes perfectly, and the March wind had given her cheeks a healthy glow.

"Have you done any office work at all?" he asked suddenly.

"A long time ago," she answered, not so winded anymore. "I worked as a legal secretary in my husband's office. I'm afraid my typing is very rusty."

Nat's face lit up. "A lawyer's office. Hey, that's great. That's the kind of experience this job needs."

"What do you mean?" Margaret said, startled. "What kind of agency are you? It doesn't say on the door."

"Oh, I'm sorry." He rummaged through the papers once again and came up with a grubby business card, which he thrust at her. "I thought you understood, I'm a detective. Nat Southby, Private Investigator," he proclaimed proudly.

She read the card and then looked at him again. He certainly didn't look like Humphrey Bogart in *The Maltese Falcon* or any of the other detectives she had seen in the movies, for that matter. He should have been leaning back in his swivel chair, his .38 revolver in a shoulder holster, and his feet on the desk, a drink in one hand and a cigarette in the other, staring defiantly into her eyes. Instead, Nat was somewhat overweight, probably in his mid-fifties, dressed in baggy grey slacks and a blue-striped shirt—a nondescript blue-and-red tie lay on the desk—with an ash-spotted, brown tweed sports jacket completing his ensemble. There was no drink and no gun.

"Don't look the part, eh?" he said with a smile, which lit up his plump face. His brown eyes twinkled out of the creases at their corners.

Margaret blushed, and to hide her confusion, asked, "What kind of investigative work do you do, Mr. Southby?"

"I take on anything. Business espionage, stolen goods, deadbeats, missing persons, fraud. You name it and I'll have a stab at it. Don't touch divorce, though." He paused for breath. "I also do a lot of leg work for different law firms. That's why I said your experience would come in useful."

"But that was years ago," she said in alarm, "before I had my two daughters. And they're in their twenties now."

"It'll come back," he said confidently. "It's like riding a bicycle. Now, let's have some particulars, such as . . . are you still married? I mean, divorced or anything?"

"I'm married."

"What about your girls? Still live at home?"

"One's married and the other's a nurse at the Royal Columbian Hospital in New Westminster."

"And your husband's a lawyer, eh? Criminal, I suppose?"

"Corporate. He's a partner in Snodgrass, Crumbie and Spencer."

"Oh yes, I've heard of them, though they're not one of the firms I work for." Nat rose from his chair. "I really don't know what else to ask you," he said. "I started this agency five years ago, you see, but the office help I've had up to now's been a disaster."

"What would I have to do?" Margaret asked.

"Come into the outer office and I'll show you," he answered, leading the way. "It'll be, you know—taking phone calls, typing up reports. Things like that." He walked over to the two filing cabinets. "These contain all the files on my clients."

Margaret sat down tentatively at the scratched wooden desk and took in the matching wooden filing trays, which were overflowing with letters and documents. "Is all this to go into those filing cabinets too?"

"Yeah," he answered. "You can see things have sort of gotten out of hand. I've tried a series of girls, but since it's just a part-time job, it attracts mostly young ones fresh out of school and on their way to something more permanent."

"And the hours are from nine to one?"

"That's right. Yeah. Will you give it a try?"

She got up from the desk and walked over to one of the

windows to look down at the busy street, and then back at his earnest face. "Yes," she said at last. "I can't promise miracles. But I'll give it a try."

"Could you start right away—say, tomorrow?" he asked hopefully.

"Well... I don't..." Then she nodded.

"Nine o'clock?"

"Well, yes. All right, I'll be here."

A half hour later, she sat sipping a cup of tea in the Aristocrat Restaurant on the corner of Broadway and Granville. *Margaret, what have you done...? How can I tell Harry about this?* The waitress placed a sandwich in front of her, and Margaret absentmindedly took a bite. *I didn't ask how much it paid. Harry will never approve... his wife working in a seedy office. And a detective's office at that.* She was still turning the problem over in her head as she slipped behind the wheel of her Morris to drive home.

The solution came to her as she was fumbling for her keys to the front door. *Why tell him at all? Just keep the whole thing to myself. It'll save all those I-told-you-sos if I should fall flat on my face.*

HARRY AWOKE THE next morning to the smell of brewing coffee. He realized that Margaret must have risen early, and as he struggled out of bed and made his way to the bathroom, he peered over the banister and was surprised to see her fully dressed in a navy-blue skirt and a cashmere twin-set in a pretty shade of coral. Before going downstairs, he showered, shaved and dressed, and when he descended to the kitchen, he found her already sitting at the table, sipping a glass of orange juice.

"You're up early," he commented as he sat down and picked up his morning newspaper. "Off somewhere?"

"Thought I'd spend my birthday money." She felt a telltale blush starting, but she had no need to worry, as Harry was already immersed in his paper and munching on a piece of toast. Quietly, she picked up her plate and cup, put them in the sink and started for the stairs.

Harry looked up. "Mmm...sorry, dear. Where did you say you were going?"

"Shopping," she answered shortly.

"Have a nice morning, then," he said, before sticking his nose back into his paper. "Going to spend my gift on something pretty?" But Margaret could see he didn't really expect an answer, as he was totally engrossed in the financial section.

THIS TIME MARGARET was lucky and found a parking place quite close to the office; to her relief, she was five minutes early. She hesitated at the door before pushing it open.

"You're here. Great!" her new boss greeted her with an affable smile. "I was afraid you'd have second thoughts."

She shook her head, and slipping her coat off, looked for someplace to hang it.

"Here, give it to me," Nat said, taking it from her. "You can use this little closet for your things."

"You know," Margaret said, "I almost did."

"Almost did what?"

"Have second thoughts about coming this morning. I don't know that I'll be able to handle the job to your satisfaction."

Nat laughed. "You'll be fine," he said. "In fact, you can get the hang of things right away. I have to go out."

"Go out?" Margaret was horrified at the thought of being left in sole charge. "What will I do if the phone rings or if someone comes in?"

"Don't worry," he said as he struggled into his overcoat. "If the phone rings, just take a message. Putter around. You can get acquainted with the office this morning." Nat opened the door.

"Find out where everything is. In fact, you might as well make a list of the things you'll need to get us properly organized."

"But Mr. Southby..."

"I'll be back in a couple of hours," he called out as he bounded down the hall to the stairs.

She walked slowly over to the desk and sat down. Then, pulling open the top drawer, she examined the sorry state of accumulated mess. Within minutes she had a pile of candy wrappers, broken pens, pencils and bent paper clips on the desk. Then, with a determined jerk, she yanked the drawer completely out and gave it a bang against the side of the wastepaper basket, making a clean sweep of it.

The telephone rang.

As she reached for the handset, she tried to manoeuvre the drawer back into its slot with the other hand. The drawer jammed. Another push and a sharp jerk sent the telephone flying onto the floor with a crash.

She walked around to the front of the desk and picked it up. "Southby's Investigations," she said, trying to sound as if nothing unusual had happened.

There was a slight pause. "Mr. Southby?" a man's voice asked.

"He's out. I mean, he's just left." Then she remembered. "Can I take a message?"

A scratching noise on the outer door distracted her from the call, and as she turned toward the sound, she watched in fascination as the handle slowly turned. "When will he be in?" the man on the phone persisted.

"I'm... uh... not sure," Margaret answered. The door had inched open a little more, and she could now see four gnarled fingers slipping around the edge. "He said about a couple of hours." The door suddenly flew fully open, and there, clinging to the frame and gasping for breath, was a wizened old man. "You're sure I can't take a message?" Margaret added, trying desperately to keep her mind on the man at the other end of the line.

"No. I'll call back."

She replaced the receiver and looked enquiringly at the old man.

"Elevator . . . not working," he wheezed. He tottered over to a chair and sank into it.

"Are you all right?" she asked him. "Can I get you a drink of water?"

"You should get that elevator fixed," he answered, slowly unwinding a red woollen scarf from his neck. "Those stairs are a killer." He took off his glasses and wiped them with a grubby handkerchief. "She's gone again," he said dabbing his eyes.

"Who's gone again?"

"My Emily, of course. She left two nights ago," he answered, blowing his nose loudly into the handkerchief. He then gave his eyes another swipe and stuffed the offensive piece of rag into his overcoat pocket. "I've come to get Mr. Southby to find her. Like last time."

Margaret rummaged through the pile on the desk, looking for a piece of paper and a useable stub of pencil.

"When did you see her last?" she asked, pencil poised over the paper.

"You don't listen. I told you . . . night before last."

"Can I have your name, Mr. . . . ?" she asked.

"What for? Southby knows me."

"But I haven't had that pleasure," she answered through gritted teeth. "If you give me your name, I can then pass it on to Mr. Southby when he comes in."

"Oh, all right. It's Bradshaw. Ernie Bradshaw," he answered. "But you're just wasting time asking all these damn fool questions."

"Perhaps you could give me a description," she said as she wrote *Missing Person* at the top of the piece of paper. "Now, what's the colour of her hair and eyes? And then perhaps you could tell me her size and anything else that would be helpful in finding her." She sat back, feeling quite professional for asking such pertinent questions.

"I told you, Southby knows all about..." The look on Margaret's face stopped him short. "Her hair's white and she's got sort of blue eyes." He paused for breath. "And she's a bit on the heavy side. Should cut her food down."

"Perhaps she went to visit a friend," Margaret said slowly. She was puzzling over the bit about *cutting down the food*.

"She went to the McCreedys' place awhile ago, but they kicked her out. She wouldn't go back there."

"Kicked her out?" Margaret said in a shocked voice. "Why would they do that?"

"You don't know the McCreedys."

"Perhaps she's not very happy?"

"Not happy? My Emily? Of course she's happy."

"But if she keeps leaving you..." Margaret was beginning to feel out of her depth.

"How can you say she's not happy?" Mr. Bradshaw's eyes began to water, and he added in a choked-up voice, "Don't I give her everything she wants?"

Margaret quickly changed the subject. "Have you thought about giving her a night out?"

"A night out?" The old man looked at her incredulously. "Night out! What would I do that for?"

"Well, if your wife keeps..."

"My wife?" he butted in. "What do you mean, my wife?"

"Uh... your girlfriend, then?"

"Are you crazy?"

"Who in heaven's name is Emily, then?" Margaret said in exasperation.

"My cat, of course," he replied scornfully. "Don't you know nothing?"

"Your cat!" She suppressed an overwhelming desire to laugh. "I'm sorry, Mr. Bradshaw, but you see, this is my first day, and I don't know Mr. Southby's clients yet. Give me your telephone number and I'll make sure he calls you as soon as he comes in."

"He's already got it." He stood up and rebuttoned his coat. "Just make sure you tell him." And muttering to himself, he went out.

After the door closed, Margaret put her head down on the typewriter and laughed until tears ran down her face. "A cat!" she spluttered. "My heavens, a cat."

The urgent ringing of the phone pulled her together.

"Southby's Investigations."

"You're new. Who are you?"

"Yes. Can I help you?"

"You sure can. First of all, what's your name?"

"Mrs. Spencer," she answered stiffly. "And yours is Mr. . . . ."

"Well, Mrs. Spencer," he mimicked her, "give my pal Southby a message. Pink Lady, third, Saturday. Got that?"

"And your name?" she insisted.

"Just tell him Prout called. Prout the Tout—he'll know." And he burst into raucous laughter at his own joke.

"I'll see he gets the message, Mr. Prout," she said primly after the laughter had subsided.

"You wanna place a bet yourself?"

"No, thank you," she answered and firmly replaced the receiver.

Margaret got through the rest of the morning with no further distractions. She cleaned out the desk, typed out a list of supplies she would need and made herself a cup of coffee, having found a fairly new and reasonably clean coffee pot and a hot plate under the debris on a small table beside the filing cabinets. Nat returned at twelve o'clock.

"How's everything?" he asked cheerily. "No problems, I guess, eh?"

"Mr. Southby, do you happen to know a Mr. Bradshaw?"

"Old Ernie. Sure. What's he want?"

"He's under the impression that you'll find a cat for him."

"Not that blasted cat again!" Nat took his coat off. "This is supposed to be a detective agency, not a lost and found for cats. Anything else?"

"A man called just after you left this morning, but he wouldn't leave his name. Said he'd call back."

"Okay. Did you make a list of office supplies?" he asked.

Margaret handed him the list.

"I'm meeting a client for lunch in thirty minutes," Nat said, looking at his watch. "Why don't you leave at the same time and slip over to the office supply store across the street. Just bill it." As Nat reached the doorway, he turned and threw a set of keys to her. "Here, these are for you," he said.

At twelve-thirty, Margaret knocked on Southby's office door. "I'm leaving now," she said.

He opened the door, shrugging into his coat. "See you in the morning," he said cheerfully.

"Oh, I forgot to tell you. Another man called—Prout. Prout the Tout, he said. He told me to tell you Pink Lady, Saturday, third. Does that mean anything to you?"

Nat laughed. "He's got to be kidding. I wouldn't touch that nag for all the tea in China."

THE NEXT MORNING, as Harry put down his newspaper to butter his toast, he glanced over at Margaret. "I don't remember seeing that suit before." Then he frowned. "Are you going out again?"

"I thought I'd go into town since it's such nice weather," Margaret answered as she stacked the breakfast dishes. *How long will I be able to keep this up?*

"It's unusual for you to go out three days in a row," he persisted.

"For God's sake, Harry, what does it matter?" she snapped, but the look on his face made her feel guilty. "Oh, I'm sorry. I'm just a bit jumpy lately."

"What you need is a change," he said, as he neatly folded his newspaper. "Perhaps I can manage to take a couple of days off when the next long weekend comes around."

"That would be nice," she said as she reached for a clean dishtowel and began to wipe the crockery. "We could both do with a change."

"I'm going, Margaret." She came out of her reverie to realize that Harry was waiting at the front door for his briefcase. "That's the second time I've called you," he said in an aggrieved voice, as she dutifully handed it to him.

"Sorry, Harry. My mind was on something else."

He bent and kissed her proffered cheek. "Shouldn't be too late tonight," he said as she closed the door on him.

It only took a few minutes to fly upstairs and straighten the bed. She grabbed her purse and raincoat from where she'd left them on the hall chair, and then practically ran through the front door, slamming it behind her before jumping into her waiting Morris.

That was nice of Harry to leave the garage door open for me, she thought as she backed out of the garage.

THERE WAS A NEAT PILE of new stationery waiting on her desk, and she was happily putting it away in the clean drawers when Nat Southby came in. "Hope that's everything you ordered," he said as he made for his own office.

"Yes, thank you," she answered, giving him a shy smile.

The phone rang shrilly, punctuating the moment.

"Southby's Investigations."

"Did you tell Southby about my Emily gone missing?" She immediately recognized the querulous voice of Ernie Bradshaw.

"Yes, Mr. Bradshaw."

"You sure you told him? You didn't forget?"

"No. I didn't forget. He will call you as soon as he can," she said firmly as she replaced the phone.

"Who was that on the phone?" Nat asked.

"Mr. Bradshaw. He wanted to make sure I'd told you about his cat."

"Oh, hell, I guess I'll have to call Violet."

"Violet?"

"Violet Larkfield. Loves cats and thinks no one else can take care of them properly, especially Ernie Bradshaw. I expect she's got Emily again."

A short while later, Margaret heard Nat on the phone. "Mrs. Larkfield? Nat Southby here... Yes, fine, thank you... Have you seen old Ernie's cat lately...? You have, eh...? Come on, Mrs. Larkfield, it could hardly be lost. It only lives a couple of blocks away... Yes, okay. Well, would you hang onto it until I can pick it up? Thanks."

"Margaret," he called out. "How'd you like to do me a favour and go and pick up that bloody cat from Violet Larkfield's? Ernie only lives a couple of streets over, but he's afraid of Violet and won't go and get the damn thing. It won't take you too far out of your way. You'll find both the addresses on file."

Margaret arose from her desk and walked into Southby's office. "Mr. Southby," she said icily, "I was employed to do *office* work. Do you usually ask your staff to pick up lost cats?"

He looked up at her in surprise and laughed. "Not usually.

But this isn't your usual type of office. Look, I'm sorry, I know it's a pain, but you'd do me a great favour if you'd pick up the animal, then whip it over to Ernie and collect the usual ten-dollar fee."

"A ten-dollar fee for returning a cat?" Margaret said indignantly. "Do you mean to say you actually charge the poor old man? That doesn't seem very honest to me, Mr. Southby."

"But that's business, Maggie," he answered with a grin. "My business, anyway. Hey! That's it."

"What's it?" Margaret asked.

"Your name, of course. Maggie. Much better than Margaret."

"But I like my name!"

"No. Too elegant for this place. Maggie it is."

"But . . ."

"So that's settled then," Nat said, picking up a sheet of paper. "Call yourself a cab and then leave a bit early, okay?" He picked up some handwritten pages from his desk. "Here, these are some notes to type up on a new client. He phoned yesterday afternoon."

"It must have been that rather rude man who wouldn't leave his name," she answered, taking the pages from him. "And Mr. Southby," she added, turning to go out of his office, "I have my own car, thank you, and I still don't think picking up cats should be part of my job." She closed his door none too gently behind her.

Nat grinned as he made a grab for the pile of papers that tried to take off in the sudden draft. *She'll do, if she sticks around . . . she'll do just fine.*

What cheek! Margaret fumed as she rolled a piece of paper into her typewriter. *Picking up stray cats. Who does he think I am?* She smoothed out the piece of paper that Nat had given her. *He ought to do his own dirty work.*

Phillip Collins, she read. Twenty-five foot, four-seater Chris-Craft Sportsman. Name: *Seagull*, inboard engine, missing five days. Police not informed. WHY NOT? Nat had underlined these two words heavily.

She was inserting the newly typed paper into a buff folder when her boss came out of his office.

"What about a nice cup of coffee?" he asked.

Margaret pushed herself roughly away from her desk.

"No, no. Don't get up," he added hurriedly. "I was offering. I'll get it."

"Well, thanks," she replied, relaxing a little. "I could do with one, actually." She knew he was trying to make up for asking her to get Bradshaw's cat, and she hid a smile as he busied himself with the coffee pot.

"It's not that I don't want to get the cat myself," he explained as he handed the coffee to her. "It's just that I'm pushed for time today. I have an appointment with Phillip Collins at eleven, and then I'm having lunch with George Sawasky, my old partner—a business lunch," he intoned quickly.

"That's all right, Mr. Southby, I'll get the cat for you." Margaret felt that she'd been neatly outmanoeuvred. "Just this once," she added. She looked at the clock on the wall. "And if you've an appointment at eleven with this Mr. Collins, he's ten minutes late."

As if on cue, the door opened and a tall, lean and tanned man walked in. Margaret put him in his mid-forties.

"Mr. Collins?" Nat asked, extending his hand. "Won't you come into my office?" He turned to his new secretary. "Will you please bring your notebook, Maggie."

"So you've had a boat stolen?" Nat said after everyone was seated. "Why not call the police?"

"It's a bit awkward, Mr. Southby. Not only is my boat missing, but my wife's young brother has gone missing, too."

"Do you think he's taken the boat?"

"I've let him use it a couple of times. But he runs around with a rotten bunch." Collins shifted uncomfortably in his seat. "My wife's been after me not to bring the police in. At least, not unless we have to."

"When did you realize the boat and your brother-in-law were missing?" Nat looked up from the piece of paper in front of him, where he'd been doodling kites and cubes.

"Five days ago. Larry had asked if he could borrow it, but I refused. He'd left it in such a mess the previous time, y'see."

"Where do you keep the boat?"

"At the Osprey Harbour Yacht Club. You must know it, out in West Vancouver."

"Sure, I've heard of it," Nat replied dryly. "You asked around the club?"

"Naturally," Collins answered stiffly. "I'm not stupid, Mr. Southby. That's the first thing I did. No one remembers seeing Larry take off." He reached inside his jacket and drew out a snapshot. "But you'd hardly expect them to notice, would you? With all the coming and going in a yacht club." He extended the picture to the detective. "That's what she looks like."

The picture showed Collins with a small blond woman, much younger than himself, standing on a dock beside a sleek blue and white runabout. The name *Seagull* was lettered on her bow.

"She looks very new," Nat commented.

"She's a couple of years old, but I take good care of her," Collins answered. "That's my wife standing in front of her," he added, holding out his hand for the picture.

"Could I keep this for awhile?" Nat asked.

Phillip Collins hesitated, and then nodded. "All right, if it will help get her back. That boat's worth twenty grand."

"I'd like some more details on your brother-in-law. Address, habits, friends. That kind of thing."

Collins thought for a short while and then said, "He's twenty-two, single, has an apartment over in Richmond, and works in a used car lot on No. 3 Road—it's also in Richmond."

"Does he live alone?"

"As far as I know," Collins answered shortly. "I'll kill that little bugger when I get my hands on him." He stood up. "Anything else you want to know?"

"Well, give Mrs. Spencer Larry's full address and place of work, where you work and a telephone number where we can reach you." Nat stood up. "I'll also need the boat's registration number and berth number at the club. Then I'll start making enquiries and get back to you as soon as possible."

"Do you think it will be necessary to bring the police into this, Mr. Southby?" Collins asked.

"We'll be as discreet as possible. I was on the force myself, and I know my way around without making too many waves." Nat shook hands and nodded toward Margaret. "Now if you'd just be good enough to give my secretary here all the details, we'll get on it."

Collins followed her out of Southby's office, and a short time later the outside door closed with a click. Nat opened his own door, and crossing Margaret's office to look out of the window, he gave a low whistle.

"Wow," he said softly. "Would you look at that baby."

She joined him at the window and looked down to the street below. Collins was slipping behind the wheel of a silver-grey Jaguar. "All that on soap!" she said incredulously. "Imagine that."

"Soap?" Nat asked, mystified. "What do you mean, soap?"

"Oh, didn't you know?" she replied with an impudent grin. "The Sudsy Specialty Soaps Company. They sell all kinds of cleaning materials as well as soap."

"Never heard of it," her boss replied.

"I received a gift package of their products through the mail once. It's surprising how very good it is."

"See how useful you are already?" Nat said with a grin. "You got all that valuable information about a client without me having to say a word."

"His father actually owns the company. Phillip Collins is the vice-president," she added.

"And how did you deduce that piece of information?"

"He gave me this," she answered with a laugh, and handed him a black-and-gold embossed business card.

Instead of being peeved at Margaret's little joke, Nat seemed pleased by it. "I knew I was doing the right thing in hiring you," he said, grinning.

CHAPTER THREE

Margaret drove to the Kitsilano address that she had found for Violet Larkfield in the files, and parked her car outside a grey stucco house with white trim. She could see a tangle of lilac, cedar and holly branches poking through the broken palings of the tall wooden fence that enclosed the property. The wooden gate protested when she pushed it open to walk up the stone-flagged path.

She paused to look at a colourful clump of mauve crocus that nestled beside the footpath. Glancing around the corner of the house toward the backyard, she could see daffodils in bud beneath the bare branches of the gnarled oak and two maple trees. *How very pleasing,* she thought, and turned to climb the three stone steps to the front door. To her astonishment, the door was suddenly jerked open.

"What do you want?"

In the doorway stood a tall gaunt woman dressed in a brown tweed skirt and a beige sweater. Her iron-grey hair was pulled back into an untidy bun. "What do you want?" she repeated, her steely blue eyes fixed on Margaret.

"I've ... uh ... I've come about the cat."

"What cat?"

"Mr. Bradshaw's cat."

The woman bent down and picked up the tabby that was winding between her legs. "I thought that Southby feller was coming for it."

"He sent me instead." Margaret felt her cheeks flush.

"Why?"

"I'm his assistant."

The woman looked Margaret up and down and grudgingly opened the door a bit wider. "Suppose you'd better come in." She turned and led the way into a large, over-furnished room.

The room's inhabitants, Margaret realized, caused the distinct odour of cat. On every available chair, table and cushion sat a cat. And in one corner, a pole had been fixed from floor to ceiling with five padded platforms. On every platform was a cat.

A large Siamese on the top platform slowly got to its feet, fixed its china-blue eyes on Margaret, arched its back, stretched its legs and hissed. Then, with a blood-curdling yowl, it sprang through the air and landed on Margaret's shoulder. She shrieked and tried to push the animal off. Giving her an extra dig with its claws, the cat leapt onto the back of the sofa, from where it eyed her with contempt.

"There, there, Satan my pet. Did she frighten you, then?" Mrs. Larkfield scooped the cat into her arms. "You should learn to have more self-control," she said, turning on Margaret. "Cats are very sensitive, you know."

"I didn't do a damned thing to it!" Margaret replied, rubbing her neck. "Which one's Mr. Bradshaw's cat?"

"I'll have to go and find her," Mrs. Larkfield answered, replacing the Siamese on its perch. "You can sit down if you want." She turned and walked out of the room.

Better said than done. With one eye on the Siamese, Margaret walked warily around the room, wondering which cat to evict, until she saw a small grey kitten curled up on an armchair. *At least it's not likely to retaliate.* Gingerly, she picked the kitten up, and to her relief, it began to purr. She sat down with it on her lap.

The stuffiness of the room and the quietness seemed to close in on her. Suddenly, the ornate clock on the mantlepiece striking one o'clock shattered the silence, giving the full Westminster chimes. She looked around at the cats, but they sat as still as statues, all staring back at her.

"Well, kitty," she said softly, "at least *you* don't seem to mind me holding you."

The kitten stretched its claws and dug them into Margaret's leg, kneading in ecstasy. Carefully unhooking them, she stroked its head. *Where is that dratted woman?*

"Don't be so stupid!" she heard Violet Larkfield's sharp voice say. "You're always picking on him."

"For God's sake," a man's voice answered, "keep your voice down."

Her curiosity aroused, Margaret got up from her chair, placed the kitten on its cushion and then walked quietly toward the door, but all she could hear was a low muttering. The voices stopped and a door banged shut. The note of a powerful car engine made her walk quickly to the window that overlooked the back of the house. It was then that she realized that the house had a driveway, but its approach was from a side street. She was just in time to see a flash of silver as a car pulled away from the garage and disappeared down the street. *That's odd. I've seen that car before.*

There was a cough behind her, and Margaret whirled to see Violet Larkfield standing in the doorway, holding a wicker cat basket. A white Persian cat was trying its best to poke its paws out through the door of the basket.

"Enjoying my view?" she asked sarcastically. "This is what you came for, isn't it? And," the woman continued, thrusting the basket into Margaret's arms, "you can tell that Ernie Bradshaw that I want the cage back."

"I'm sure he will gladly return it to you," Margaret answered tersely as she walked toward the front door.

"And another thing, you tell him from me that there won't be a next time. She comes back here, it's here she stays." And she practically shoved Margaret through the door and slammed it shut.

"Now to get you back to your grateful owner," Margaret said through gritted teeth. The basket seemed to weigh a ton, the door was loose, and with the cat yowling inside, she found it hard to carry it in a dignified manner toward her car. She finally stopped to put a bobby pin on the latch, frustrated and certain the odious woman was watching her every step from the house.

"Pipe down!" she told the cat as she opened the rear door and practically threw the basket onto the back seat. "You just wait until I see you in the morning, Mr. Southby," she muttered under her breath. "No wonder he didn't want to collect the wretched animal."

Ernie Bradshaw lived on Eighth Avenue, just two streets over from the Larkfield residence. It was starting to rain as she walked up the broken concrete path that led to a scarred brown front door. She set the basket containing the cat on the ground and looked for a doorbell. There wasn't one. She banged on the door with her fist. Except for Emily's plaintive meows, all was silent.

"That's all I need, for him to be out," she said angrily and banged again. This time there was a faint shuffling noise and sounds of chains and locks being undone. The door opened a crack, just enough for her to see Ernie's surly face peering at her through the opening.

"You've got her then?"

"Yes, Mr. Bradshaw." She forced the door open and plunked the basket at Ernie's feet. "Mrs. Larkfield found her wandering in her garden and took her in. And she wants this basket back."

"Catnapped, more like."

Her self-control snapped. "Mr. Bradshaw," she said haughtily, "I would suggest that you begin to take more care of your pet."

"Hey! You can't talk to me like that . . ."

She started to turn away from him in disgust. "If she disappears again, you know where to look for her, don't you? Oh," she added, "that will be ten dollars." Gone were her scruples about taking money from a poor, lonely old man. In fact, she felt it should have been double.

Grumbling, Ernie shuffled back into the darkness of the narrow passageway to reappear a short time later, carrying a handful of crumpled bills. He thrust them into her hands, saying, "Highway robbery I calls it. And I'm going to complain to Mr. Southby about your attitude."

"I hope you do, Mr. Bradshaw," Margaret Spencer said as she walked back to the Morris. "I hope you do."

MARGARET KICKED OFF her shoes inside her front door, walked through to the kitchen and dumped her bag of groceries on the counter. "Damn!" The phone that had been ringing all the time she had stood in the rain, struggling with her door key, was now silent. She shook the water off her coat and hung it over the back of a chair.

"Hot soup!" She reached into a cupboard and took down a can of tomato soup. Using one hand to stir the pan of soup, she used the other to rub vigorously at her wet hair with a towel. "I'm starved."

The telephone shrilled again.

"Hello."

"Is that you, Margaret?" Harry's petulant voice came over the wire. She reached over and turned down the burner.

Who else would it be? Margaret felt her irritation rise. "Of course it's me, Harry."

"Where have you been? I've been trying to reach you all day."

"Out!" she answered shortly. "Is there anything wrong?"

"I have to go to Toronto tomorrow on the Harris case. I've got to catch the seven o'clock plane in the morning."

"How nice for you!"

"You'll need to pack a bag for me."

"How long are you going for this time, Harry?"

"About five days." Margaret did some mental arithmetic. No Harry until next Thursday. "I'll be home around six," he continued.

She started to put the phone down.

"And, Margaret . . ."

"Oh, sorry. I've got to go, Harry. My soup is boiling over."

"It's just that I'm sorry about Saturday night."

"Saturday night?" she asked, puzzled.

"You know. The birthday dinner I promised you."

"Oh, that. It's all right, Harry. Another time."

She poured the soup into a bowl, placed it on a tray, tucked *The Province* newspaper under her arm and carried the tray into the living room, where she sank into her favourite armchair to enjoy her lunch.

The telephone rang again.

"Now what does he want?"

She reached for the extension.

"Hello, Maggie? Nat Southby. Wanted to see if you got home safely after meeting our Violet."

She took a deep breath. "Margaret," she corrected him. "And I was going to call you about that woman."

"Thought you would. Quite a character, isn't she?"

"Mr. Southby, you employed me as office help. I do not consider calling on people like Mrs. Larkfield or Mr. Bradshaw office work."

There was a pause on the other end of the line. "You sound upset."

"Upset! I've never met two such objectionable people in my entire life!"

"You want to tell me what happened?" He sounded resigned.

Margaret explained in detail. "And all over a damned cat," she finished up. "It was so ridiculous." When she stopped speaking, she could hear an odd rumbling sound coming over the phone. She felt herself getting red in the face.

"Are you laughing at me, Mr. Southby?"

"I'm sorry, Maggie. I was just imagining your face when you saw all those damn cats."

Margaret's resolution to be stern crumbled, and she too started to laugh.

"Have a nice weekend." He was still laughing when she replaced the receiver.

And she did have a nice weekend. She found herself singing while she cleaned house and got her clothes ready for the following week. Suddenly, she had a purpose in life, something that had been lacking for far too long.

Nat had a very busy weekend. Saturday morning found him in the vicinity of the Osprey Harbour Yacht Club, looking for one of his old school pals.

"Nat Southby! What you doing in this neck of the woods?"

Nat looked up at the sound of the familiar voice. "Cubby! Just the man I was coming to see."

John Cuthbertson gave a final polish to the brass rails on the sleek mahogany-and-teak forty-five-foot cruiser and leaned toward Nat. "What can I do for you?"

"You've come up in the world, haven't you?" the detective asked, jerking his head toward the boat. "Bit better than that old tub you used to call a yacht."

"Business has been kind to me," Cubby answered and winked. "Got time for a beer?" He picked up the half full bottle of beer that was waiting on the dock and waved it at Southby.

"Thanks, but I'll take a rain check."

"Well, here's mud in your eye," Cubby said, swallowing the rest of the contents of the bottle before coming up for air. "What are you doing here? Bought yourself a boat?"

"No such luck. My business doesn't pay like yours."

"What kind of business are you in? I know you chucked the force."

"I thought you knew. I started my own investigation service about six years ago. Wouldn't happen to know a character named Phillip Collins, would you?"

Cubby scratched his chin thoughtfully. "Can't say I do off-hand. Keeps a boat here, does he?"

"He did up to last week. A twenty-five-foot four-seater Chris-Craft. It's gone missing."

"Insurance scam?"

"Too early to tell at this stage. Do me a favour and listen around, will you? Let me know if you hear anything." Nat handed him one of his business cards. "If I'm not there, my Girl Friday will take a message."

"Okay," Cubby said as he slipped the card into his shirt pocket.

"Where can I find the caretaker?"

"Over there," Cuthbertson answered, pointing to a small office on the dock. "Name's McNab. But I doubt you'll find him this time of the day."

"I'll give it a try, anyway." As he made his way toward McNab's office, he couldn't help feeling a twinge of envy, seeing all the shining boats bobbing up and down on their moorings. *Just look at all that money. Ah, well, someday, me boy, someday!*

He found McNab sitting behind a battered oak desk, a weather-beaten man in his late sixties, puffing away at a smelly briar pipe. "And what can I do for ye, laddie?" he asked when Nat poked his head in the door.

Nat smoothed the edges of another of his grubby business cards and handed it over. "I'm making enquiries about Phillip Collins' boat, *Seagull*."

"Are ye now?" McNab answered, not bothering to look at the card. "Sit ye doon."

"You've heard that it's disappeared?"

"Couldn't help knowing about it," McNab said, reaching for another match. "Yon chappie Collins came in here shouting fit to bust. Tried to tell him it's nothing to do with me, but he wouldna' listen."

"Did he mention his suspicions regarding his brother-in-law?"

"Did mention something like that." He leaned back in his chair, closed his eyes and puffed contentedly on his pipe.

"What did he say?" Nat tried to conceal his impatience, especially with the coming and going of the old man's Scottish brogue.

McNab slowly opened his eyes. "Larry took it, of course. But as I told him, he should've padlocked it up in the first place."

Nat stood up. "You'll let me know if you hear anything?"

"Ay, I'll do that right enough." Nat had started for the door when McNab added, "But ye know, it's not the first time."

"What do you mean?" Nat turned abruptly. "What's not the first time?"

"Not the first time that young punk took the *Seagull*. In fact, he takes it out quite regular."

"They must have been on fairly good terms, then, if Collins has been letting him use it."

"Don't know about that. Matter of fact, I saw them having a good set-to."

"When was that?"

"About a couple of days before the boat went missing."

"Did you hear what it was about?"

"No. They shut up when they saw me. It was getting dark and I was making my rounds, see."

"You didn't hear anything they said?" Nat persisted.

"I thought I heard Collins saying something about risk, but I could've been mistaken. Like I told ye, laddie, they shut up right quick when they saw me."

"Could I ask you a favour, Mr. McNab? Would you show me where the *Seagull* was berthed?"

McNab heaved himself from his seat with surprising agility. "Follow me then, laddie." He led the way outside, down one of the slatted ramps and onto the float. "Over there," said McNab. "Number twenty." And leaving Nat standing, he walked back to his office.

Next to number twenty, a young woman was busy passing supplies from a wheelbarrow to a man on a boat. "Hi, there!" Nat called to them. "*Seagull's* usually berthed here, isn't it?" He indicated the empty space next to them.

"Yeah," the man answered. He leaned over the side of the boat and took a box from his companion. "But she's not here now. Gimme the gas cans next, Sylvia."

"I can see that," Nat answered. "How long she been gone?"

"Don't know. Dammit, Sylvia!" He turned angrily to the woman, who was now struggling with a large gas can. "What the hell are you doing? You nearly dumped the bloody thing in the drink."

"Oh, shut up and get on with it," she answered as she handed the can over and bent to get another one from the wheelbarrow.

Nat intercepted, took the can from her hands and swung it toward her partner.

"Can you remember when you last saw the *Seagull*?" he asked her.

"Must have been at least a week ago." She stretched her back. "Wouldn't you say, honey?"

"Yeah, I guess," 'Honey' answered. "It was before we had that big blow, anyway."

"That's right." Sylvia turned to Nat. "That was last Tuesday. We'd come down to see if *Flying Fancy* was okay, and *Seagull* was gone then." She handed the last cartons up to her husband.

"For God's sake," the man said irritably, "go get the rest of the stuff from the truck. We'll never get out at this rate."

"I'm going as fast as I can," she answered, and picking up the handles of the wheelbarrow, she trundled back up the walkway. Nat quickly caught up to her.

"Thanks for your help," he said as he walked behind her.

"That's okay," she answered over her shoulder. "Sorry we couldn't be of more help. We're only weekenders ourselves, you know."

That ties in with Collins' statement, Nat thought after he'd left the woman. *He said the boat had been missing five days.*

"Hey, laddie."

Nat turned at the sound of McNab's voice.

"I've been waiting for ye to come back."

"What can I do for you, Mr. McNab?"

"It's what I can do for ye, laddie. Come on in a wee while." He led the way back into his snug office. "Sit ye down. I was just on the phone to me pal down at the harbour police station," he said, "to see if he knew anything about your missing boat."

"And did he?"

"No. He was right mad, too. Said he should have been notified straightaway. Especially if someone was on-board at the time."

"That was up to Collins." Nat reached into his pocket for a cigarette. "I've only just been brought in on the case."

"Stevens—the harbour police chappie—asked for you to get in touch with him. He wants a full report."

Nat got up. "You can tell him that I'll get in touch if and when I get something definite."

"Well, good luck to ye, laddie." McNab gave a hoarse chuckle. "I've got a feeling you're going to need it, dealing with those two."

"You're probably right," Nat muttered to himself as he made his way from McNab's office up to the lot where he had parked his car.

CHAPTER FOUR

Around eight o'clock that evening, it started to rain heavily. Shivering in the cold wind, Ernie Bradshaw clutched his wet overcoat closer as he probed the bushes on either side of the gate with his walking stick.

"Emily!" he whispered. "Where are you?" Tentatively, he pushed the gate open, the squeak from its rusty hinges making him pause, but after waiting for a couple of minutes, he shuffled through and into the garden. Fumbling in his overcoat pocket, he pulled out a flashlight and started up the stone-flagged path. He shone the weak beam back and forth across the wet bushes and shrubs, hissing his cat's name repeatedly as he went.

As he rounded the corner of the house, he saw light pouring from one of the main-floor windows and quickly switched off the flashlight, sidling toward the window only to realize that it was too high off the ground for him to see inside the room. Cautiously, using his flashlight again, he looked for something to stand on, but all he could find was a large clay pot containing a dead chrysanthemum. Emptying the contents onto a nearby flowerbed, Ernie placed the pot upside down below the window and gingerly climbed onto it.

"I told you! I want one thousand dollars each," Violet's voice came to him through the glass, "or I'm out."

"Calm down. You'll get the rest when the goods are delivered."

Ernie didn't recognize the man's voice, so he strained on tiptoe to see into the room. "I knew she was up to no good," he whispered to himself. The flowerpot wobbled. He grabbed at the wooden windowsill to steady himself, but felt the pot sliding under his feet, and the next moment he was falling heavily onto his knees. Shuffling to his feet, he flattened himself against the house and prayed they hadn't heard the noise, but the window was suddenly flung open.

"Who's there?" Violet demanded.

Ernie's old heart thumped, and it took all of his willpower to hold his breath and remain still.

"Must have been one of your ruddy cats," the unknown man cackled. "Don't be so nervous."

The window slammed shut.

The old man waited until he had stopped shaking before groping his way to the back of the house. A large garage with a shingle-roofed annex loomed up in the dark, and he debated using his light again. Gently, he turned the knob of the annex door. To his surprise, it was unlocked, and he took a tentative step inside. "Emily?" he called under his breath. The beam from the flashlight made no impression on the blackness within the building, but he thought he heard a movement. Taking another cautious step, his shaking hand making the feeble light dance on the walls, he called again. "Emily! Is that you?"

Hearing a whimpering sound from the back of the shed, he stepped in further. To his amazement, the beam of his flashlight caught, not his missing cat, but a young girl lying on a camp bed, a look of terror on her face. "Have you seen my Em . . . ?"

They were the last words that Ernie uttered. An iron crowbar cut him off in mid-sentence, smashing his fragile skull as easily as if it had been an egg. Ernie collapsed without making another sound, falling into a heap on the floor. As he lay in the pool of blood that now gushed from his head, carrying with it the last of his miserable life, a white cat walked over to him and rubbed against his still-twitching outstretched hand, and then, arching its back and lifting its tail high, it walked out into the night.

CHAPTER FIVE

Monday morning began cloudy, dull and grey, but to Margaret, walking from the parking lot she had discovered just a block from the office, it seemed, to the contrary, to herald the start of another exciting day. She slipped her key into the lock but found the door already open. Her boss was ahead of her.

"Hi," Southby said. "Don't take your coat off."

"Why not?"

"We're going to visit your favourite client." He zippered up his windbreaker.

"Are you, by any chance, talking about Ernie Bradshaw?" she retorted and continued taking her coat off. "If so, you don't need me."

"Well, he left an odd message with my answering service." He took the coat from her and then held it out again.

"What do you mean odd?"

"He said he's got some information—worth money, as he put it."

"Couldn't you just call him?"

"Tried that several times. No answer."

"Why do you need me? Perhaps he's just away for the weekend," she said, reluctantly slipping her arms back into the coat.

"Old Ernie? He never goes away." He held the door open for her. "Come on."

"Hasn't he got any relatives, children or something?" she asked over her shoulder as she led the way down the stairs.

"He's got one daughter that I am aware of, a Mrs. Read, but she lives over on Vancouver Island someplace."

"Then perhaps he's gone there."

"Nah. He wouldn't spend the money for the ferry or leave his precious cat. He opened the outside door. "Here, we'll take my car."

Maggie slid into the passenger seat of the battered old Chevy. "You still haven't explained why you want me along."

"I just know how much you like Ernie," he laughed as he caught the expression on her face. "And since you started *The Case of the Missing Cat*, it's only right you should be in on the end of it."

Ernie's house looked even dingier in the dull morning light. Emily, fluffy tail flying high, walked down the path to greet them.

"Hello, Emily old girl." She bent down and stroked the cat's wet coat. "Been locked out?" Emily, purring ingratiatingly, stood on her hind legs and reached up to cling to Maggie's leg. "Down you go; your feet are wet." Gently, she pushed the cat off and followed her boss to the front door.

He knocked loudly on the door. "Come on, Bradshaw, open up." He tried the handle but the door wouldn't budge. He banged again, to no avail. "I'm going to look around the back, Maggie."

She followed him around the side of the house, and the cat followed her.

The detective stretched up to see through the window, but the dirty net curtains did their job well. "There seems to be a light on in there." He tapped on the window. "Ernie?"

Maggie tried the back door. "Here, Mr. Southby. It's open." She pushed it a bit wider and the cat slipped between her feet into the utility room. "Mr. Bradshaw," she called. She turned to her boss. "Do you think he's sick?"

"We'd better take a look."

Emily was sitting outside the closed kitchen door, waiting for someone to open it for her. Maggie scooped the cat up and turned the handle. The place was a shambles—table, chairs, crockery all smashed or overturned—and amidst the mess lay Ernie Bradshaw, face down.

"Mr. Southby," she cried out in horror. "It's Mr. Bradshaw!" Nat Southby pushed past her and knelt beside Ernie to feel for a pulse. "Is he . . . is he dead?"

"Afraid so." He stood up, pulling his frightened assistant toward him. "The skin's cold. He's been dead for some time." One of the old man's arms was stretched out above him, the stiff claw-like fingers seeming to be reaching for some unknown object. The back of his head was completely caved in, and although the wound was crusted with blood, the detective immediately noted that there was none on the floor. "Curious!" he muttered.

Maggie made a small whimpering sound, and to her boss' consternation, he felt her slipping out of his grasp. Putting his arm around her, he guided her to the small living room at the front of the house. "Sit here, Maggie. I'll get you some water." He was back within seconds, and holding her head tightly, he got her to sip from the glass.

"I'm sorry," she said after a moment, leaning back against the chair. "Who could've done such a thing?"

"I don't know," he replied grimly. "But we'll do our best to find out." He stood looking down at her. "Will you be okay while I phone the police?"

The wait seemed interminable to her. Nat Southby spent the time prowling the rest of the house. He found two bedrooms and a bathroom upstairs. One bedroom, obviously Ernie's, included an unmade bed, a dresser, its open drawers spilling clothes onto the floor, and a closet, where clothes had been roughly pulled off their hangers. The whole room looked as if it had been given a thorough going-over. The second bedroom, used for storage, contained a single bed, boxes of books, broken appliances, stacks of old newspapers and magazines, and a closet full of men's and women's clothes. Nat retraced his steps downstairs and stood in the doorway of the kitchen, looking over the mess. He felt Maggie come up beside him and place her hand on his arm. "Contrived!" he said. "That's it. It's just too damn contrived."

"What do you mean—contrived?"

"Take a look. At first glance you'd think there'd been a fierce fight, but it's only the *back* of Ernie's head that's bashed in." He felt Maggie give a violent shiver, and he began guiding her back to the living room. "You see," he continued, "if Ernie had been in a fight, he would have had other bruises and abrasions, but as far as I can tell without moving him, he hasn't." There was a sound of a siren in the distance, and he went over to the window. "Even the mess is too neat—if you can understand what I mean."

She nodded, though still somewhat unsure. "What's it like upstairs?"

"The same. I very much doubt if anything of value was taken," he finished, as a police cruiser drew up to the house. "We won't pass on my theories to our friends," he said as he walked to the front door. "Let 'em find out for themselves."

From the kitchen doorway, they watched the police officers kneel beside the body. "He's dead," said the shorter of the two. "We'd better call in." He turned to the waiting pair. "You the one that found him?"

Nat nodded. "Yes. Along with Mrs. Spencer here."

"You touch anything?"

"Only Ernie, just to make sure he was dead."

"Who are you? And what are you doing here?" the cop asked, taking out his notebook. "Let's join your lady friend in the other room and you can both do some talking."

To Maggie, the rest of the morning passed like a bad dream. The only time she'd had any dealings with the police had been over a speeding ticket, and Harry had made enough fuss over that. *My God, what will he say when he finds out that I'm mixed up in a murder?*

The cop's name turned out to be MacKenzie King, and Maggie wondered if his mother had been politically motivated. But she refrained from asking, since he didn't look like the joking kind. Soon after their interview, where everything they'd said seemed to be suspect, a police doctor and photographer arrived, and again Maggie and Nat were kept waiting in the stuffy living room.

"How long will they keep us here?" Nervous, she got up and looked out the window. A sizable crowd had already gathered on the sidewalk. "Look at them. What makes people relish trouble?"

Her boss joined her at the window. "Makes their humdrum lives a bit more interesting, I suppose. Also, it's happening to someone else."

As if to reinforce his words, the noise of the crowd intensified as an ambulance and another police car drew up.

"Oh, shit!" he exclaimed as they watched two plainclothes officers follow the ambulance attendants up the path.

"Why? What is it?"

"The one in the front, that's Farthing. He was brown-nosing his way to the top when I quit the force. And there's no love lost between us," he added grimly.

"What the hell are you doing here, Southby?" Mark Farthing looked incredulously at Nat and a very pale Maggie. "Been interfering again? Stay put. I'll talk to you later." He disappeared into the kitchen.

"He didn't seem very happy to see you," she said as she sank once again into the easy chair.

Nat Southby shrugged. "That's life."

It was almost noon before Mark Farthing returned to the living room. "Okay. I'm listening."

"Bradshaw left a message that he wanted to see me," the detective explained. "We found him dead."

"When did he call you?"

"My answering service took the call sometime over the weekend. Saturday, I think she said."

"Why call you? Did you know him?"

Nat Southby looked uncomfortable. "I . . . uh . . . sort of found his cat for him."

"His cat?" There wasn't even the ghost of a smile on Farthing's face.

"It was sort of a favour."

"I still don't understand what you're doing here. He lose the animal again?"

"No. Not as far as I know. Just said he wanted to see me. Maggie came along for the ride."

"Maggie?"

"Yes. My assistant. Mrs. Spencer here."

"I see," Farthing answered, but she didn't think he did. "Did you try to call him on the phone?" he persisted.

"Of course I did. Several times. Maggie thought he might have fallen or something, so we decided we'd better come and see if he was okay." He looked over at Maggie, whose mouth was open in astonishment. "You were right to be worried, weren't you, Maggie?"

She managed to compose her face before Farthing turned to her.

"Yes. He is . . . uh . . . was rather old and sort of tottery, you know."

"Mmm. Yes, I see."

"He didn't look at all well..." Maggie found herself prattling on.

"Well, you can go now, but you know the drill, Southby. Be prepared for us to call on you." He started for the kitchen. "Nice meeting you, Mrs. Spencer."

Maggie picked up her handbag from the floor just as Emily walked into the room. "Oh, Sergeant Farthing?"

"Yes." Farthing turned.

"The cat. What are you going to do with the cat?"

"What cat? Oh, that cat. Take it to the pound, I suppose. Why?"

"I know someone who'd look after her until Ernie's daughter can be located. Would it be okay to take her?"

"Don't see why not. One less thing for us to look after." He turned to Nat. "Oh, and just a word of warning, Southby—this is a police matter now, and just remember that you're not one of Mulligan's bright boys anymore. Don't interfere. Is that clear?"

"What's he mean—Mulligan's bright boys?" Maggie asked, scooping up Emily on the way out to the car. "You weren't mixed up in all that scandal, were you?"

"One of the reasons I left the force," he answered tersely. "Come on, let's get that damned cat into the car. And who," he continued, watching Maggie struggling with the animal, "is this wonderful person that's going to look after the prime suspect here?"

"Why, Violet Larkfield, of course," she answered with a wicked smile.

"You must be joking," he said, grinning back at her. "I thought you said you wouldn't go back there for love or money."

"Do you have any other suggestions?" she replied. "Your place, for instance?"

"No, Violet it is. But I'll wait in the car."

When they reached the Larkfield house a few minutes later,

Maggie turned to her employer. "You're a coward, Mr. Southby." She got out of the passenger seat, holding the squirming Emily tightly to her, but before pushing the gate open, she paused to look at the garden with its trees and shrubs. *There's something quite creepy about this place.* She took a big breath and a firmer hold on the cat as she approached the porch.

Violet Larkfield flung open the front door. "What do you want this time?"

Definitely not a good start. "Mrs. Larkfield, we wondered... uh... Mr. Southby wondered if you could look after Emily for awhile?"

"Why?" Violet stepped past Maggie and peered down the path toward Nat's car.

"It's Ernie. He seems to . . . ."

Violet Larkfield interrupted. "I suppose you'd better bring her in."

In the hallway, she took the cat gently into her arms and stroked its head. Emily immediately responded by pushing herself against the woman's scrawny neck and purring in ecstasy. "That's my pet then," Violet said lovingly. She turned her back on Maggie. "So why bring her to me?"

"Ernie Bradshaw has met with an accident."

"What kind of accident?"

"Well—he's dead."

"Dead? His heart give out?"

"No, not his heart. He seems to have been murdered. We... Mr. Southby and I... found him a short while ago."

"How come you found him?"

"It's a long story. Most likely it was a robbery." Maggie shifted uncomfortably. "You can blame me for bringing Emily to you. I know she likes it here and you do seem to like cats..." Her voice trailed off.

Violet looked hard at her. "How long do you expect me to keep her this time?" she said, putting Emily down on the floor.

"Until we contact Ernie's daughter, if that's alright with you?" Maggie watched Emily pad over to sniff the wicker cat basket that was on the floor. "Oh, I see Mr. Bradshaw brought your cat basket back."

"Haven't seen hide nor hair of him."

"But isn't that it over there?" Maggie said, pointing to it.

"No, I've got several of them." She opened the door. "You'd better go. Your boss is waiting."

"Everything okay?" he said as she slid into her seat.

"I suppose so," she answered absently. "It was just a little strange."

He put the car into gear and pulled away from the curb. "Violet's always strange."

"Yes. I mean no . . . It's just that I asked her if Ernie had returned the cat basket and she said he hadn't."

"Knowing Ernie, I can understand that."

"But I saw it there."

"She must have more than one."

"Yes, that's what she said, only . . . Mr. Southby, I recognized that particular basket. It's the same one I used the other day."

"You sure?"

"The opening wouldn't stay closed and I had a problem keeping Emily inside. Eventually, I jammed it shut with a bobby pin. I always have a few in my handbag."

"And?" he prompted.

"The basket in her hallway still had the bobby pin in it."

"So that means she either collected it herself or Ernie was there sometime between Friday and noon yesterday."

"Why yesterday?"

"By the look of him, he'd been dead for at least ten or twelve hours."

They drove the rest of the way back to the office in silence. "There has to be a logical explanation," she said as she got out of the car. "He probably left the basket on her doorstep. Didn't want to face her."

"Possibly," Nat said. "But why deny it's the same one?"

"Didn't want to get involved?"

He bent down and locked the car doors. "I guess you want to go home?"

"Yes, I think I will. My car's parked in the lot on the next street." She stepped off the curb. "Oh, by the way, did you hear any more from Phillip Collins?"

"No. He was supposed to call me. He may have left a message with the answering service."

"I'll see you tomorrow, then. And please, no more murders."

Nat Southby laughed. "I'll do my best. Go on. Go home and put your feet up and try and forget old Ernie. We've a busy day tomorrow."

If Maggie had bothered to glance back at her employer as she crossed the road, she would have seen a strange, bemused expression on his face as he watched her every movement. Back in his office, he relit his half-smoked cigar, leaned back in his leather chair and closed his eyes. A fit of coughing brought him abruptly upright. "Damn it," he muttered. He stubbed out the offending cigar in an oversized glass ashtray and then drew a lined pad toward him. "Gotta give those things up." He started to write.

Maggie, on the other hand, was doing her best to follow her boss' advice and put the morning's horror firmly out of her mind. *A cup of tea, a long hot bath and the rest of the day with my feet up.* Slipping her coat off and hanging it in the hall closet, she caught sight of herself in the mirror. *And a touch of makeup*, she amended.

The bath did wonders, and after lighting the living room fire, she put an LP on the turntable and then looked through a pile of library books. *It's definitely not the time for a whodunit*, she thought, and chose a light romance called *A Shining Morning*. She snuggled down into her old terry cloth robe. *Thank God, Harry won't be home for supper tonight.*

It was the insistent ringing of the doorbell that woke her.

"Blast! Who can that be?" She struggled from the chair and walked to the window. "Barbara—today of all days!"

Tall and slim, Barbara stood waiting for her mother to open the door. A gust of wind blew a strand of blonde hair into her eyes and she brushed it away with an impatient gesture.

"Barbara, how nice to see you." Margaret tried to put some enthusiasm into her voice. "Come on in, dear."

Barbara studied her mother. "Are you sick or something?"

"No, just having a rest." She led the way into the room. "Sit down by the fire. I'll make some tea and you can tell me your news."

"Can't stay long." Barbara slipped her coat off and laid it beside her on the sofa. "I called before, but there was no answer. Were you out?"

"Yes," her mother said. "I was out. Now just relax. I'll only be a minute." When Margaret returned with the tea, she saw her daughter still sitting tensely upright. *If only she'd loosen up a bit*, Margaret thought. *She's every inch her father.*

"Dad's worried about you," Barbara said in her abrupt manner.

Margaret paused in the act of passing her a cup. "Whatever for? There's lemon on the tray."

"I can see why he's worried. Just look at you! The middle of the afternoon and you're not even dressed."

"But..."

"Just because he's out of town doesn't mean that you should let yourself go."

"When did he tell you he was worried?" Margaret tried to hold onto her temper. "He never mentioned it on the phone last night."

"He called me right after speaking to you. He said you were distracted. Didn't take in anything he said." She took a sip of tea. "He says that you never listen to him these days."

He hasn't said anything worth listening to. Instantly, Margaret felt guilty for the thought.

The telephone gave a welcome jangle.

"I'll get it." Barbara reached over the back of the sofa and picked up the telephone. "I'm sorry, I think you must have the wrong number," she said. "Yes, this is 8876 . . . Yes . . ."

She turned to her mother. "Some man wants to speak to . . . Maggie!"

Margaret couldn't help grinning at the expression on her daughter's face. "That's me," she said, taking the receiver. "Hello, Mr. Southby!" She listened for awhile, then said, "Okay. I'll see you at 9:30. Bentley Street Police Station. Yes, I've got it . . . I know where it is. No, there's no need to pick me up. Bye." She replaced the phone. Barbara sat with a look of astonishment on her face.

"Who was that? What's that about a police station?"

"It was just a friend. I . . . uh . . . we were witnesses to an accident today. We have to make a statement." To Margaret's chagrin, the lie came easily.

"Oh! Is that all?" Barbara replied. But the look on her face made Margaret realize that she had only raised a new spectre in her daughter's mind.

"What time does Charles get home?" Margaret asked, to change the subject.

Barbara took the bait. "Six. Oh dear, I didn't know it was so late."

"Give him my love," Margaret said as she helped her daughter into her coat. "You'd better come over for dinner when your dad gets back."

After Barbara left, Margaret closed the door and leaned against it. *That's it. I've got to tell Harry.* She returned to the living room and sank into her chair, but her peace of mind had gone and she started to go over and over the events of the day.

AFTER TOSSING AND TURNING for hours, Margaret eventually fell into a troubled sleep, and then the weird dreams began. She found herself following the white cat along a dark, tree-lined path that suddenly opened out into a unkempt baseball field with tall grass rippling like waves in the wind. In the distance she could see a coffin with its lid open. She was terrified but felt compelled to walk toward it. As she neared the coffin, she could see the cat circling the bier. Standing on tiptoe, she looked down into the casket. Harry lay there, his eyes wide open and staring right at her. "Margaret!" he said in an authoritative voice, "Where have you been?" Then, abruptly, he sat up and reached toward her. She tried to scream, but as in most dreams, no sound came. Turning from the coffin, she began running blindly back the way she had come. But there was no escape. The heavy footsteps pounded behind her, getting closer and closer. Back through the tunnel of trees she ran, but the path was even darker now and there were golden cat's eyes glinting at her from the low branches. Suddenly, a large black Siamese, its blue eyes gleaming with hate, leapt from a branch toward her. She awoke, her mouth open in a scream, but it was the noise from the alarm clock that was ringing in her ears. She reached over to shut it off and lay back onto her pillow, heart thumping. But this time she didn't close her eyes. "I can't go on like this."

By the time the darkness made way for the day, Margaret,

now showered, dressed and with a cup of coffee in hand, allowed herself to think about the impending visit to the police station. Even though she was a law-abiding citizen, the prospect of the forthcoming interrogation was appalling to her, perhaps all the more so because of the lack of familiarity. And to make matters worse, it was another rainy day!

Her boss was waiting for her outside the precinct, and she followed him up a flight of stairs and along a dusty corridor to Mark Farthing's office. "Chin up, this is going to be rough," he said as he knocked and then opened the door.

"Ah, Southby. On time, I see. And you too, Mrs. Spencer." He reached across his very tidy desk and shook her hand. "Sit down and I'll call the steno in." He reached for the phone. After the steno arrived, Farthing led them bit by bit through the events of the two previous days. "And you still maintain you know nothing of what he wanted?"

"I've no idea," Nat Southby answered.

"Why did you wait until yesterday before you tried to call him?" Farthing persisted.

"I didn't pick up the weekend's messages until yesterday morning."

Farthing turned to Maggie. "You met Bradshaw. Did you think he had something serious on his mind when he came to your office?"

"Other than finding his cat, no."

"How long have you been working for Mr. Southby?"

"I started last week."

"And you feel you could make that assumption on such a short acquaintance?"

"Yes, I feel I could make that assumption, Sergeant Farthing. He was a very self-centred and bad-tempered old man. All he was interested in was his cat."

"Given that he was a bad-tempered man," he said, turning to Nat, "what made you two run over there so promptly?"

"For God's sake, Mark!" Nat exploded. "What makes anyone of us do such things? Call it a hunch, if you like." He stood up and glared down at Farthing. "How the hell were we to know he'd been murdered?"

"My name's Sergeant Farthing, if you don't mind," he said, glaring back. "Now cool down. You two have got yourself into this mess and you'll answer any damn questions I please to ask." He turned curtly to the steno, who was sitting with his mouth open. "You can type up those statements and have them ready for their signatures. And after you two have signed them, you're free to go."

"Have you any idea who did it?" Maggie asked as she stood up to leave.

"At this minute—no," Farthing replied. "But *we'll* be the ones finding out. Is that clear?" He reached for the telephone. "I take it you know where the duty office is?"

"Jackass!" Nat Southby said under his breath as they walked down the dark corridor.

"He certainly seems to have it in for you," Maggie answered quietly.

"Yeah! I can't quite figure out why, though. After all, he stepped into a damn good job when I left. Think he'd be pleased."

PHILLIP COLLINS WAS WAITING for them when they arrived back at the office. "I've been trying to get hold of you."

Nat led the way inside. "What can I do for you?"

"I've decided to call off your investigation."

"You've found your boat?"

"No, but my wife feels that Larry will turn up soon. Like he always does."

"Well, it's up to you, Collins. But the boat's been missing now for nearly ten days. That's a helluva spree, isn't it?"

"I'll pay you for your time so far."

"What did you say your boat's worth? Twenty grand? And you're suddenly not worried about it?"

"That's none of your business," Collins answered. "I said I want to drop the case." He arose from his chair and took out his cheque book and a gold pen. "How much do I owe you?" Nat named his figure, Collins wrote out a cheque and was gone a few moments later.

From the window they watched him get into his car.

"Of course!" she cried suddenly. "That's what's been bothering me."

"What?"

"The car. Collins' car. I've seen it before."

"Of course you have. It's the same one he was driving last week."

"I know that. But it was also at Violet Larkfield's. You know, last Friday when I went to her house. That car was in the driveway."

"There have to be a dozen Jaguars in this town."

"Not silver-grey ones. I'm sure that's the same car I saw leaving Violet Larkfield's driveway."

"Are you sure? Listen, Maggie, you've been through a rough few days," he said in a placating tone that only infuriated her. "You could be a mite overwrought and getting things a bit mixed up."

"*Mister* Southby," Maggie said witheringly, "I saw that car at Violet Larkfield's, *and*, by the way, I also saw the cat basket that Ernie had returned." She turned, sat down at her typewriter and began pounding furiously.

THAT EVENING MARGARET WAITED until she'd finished washing the supper dishes and she and Harry were seated by the living room fire, having coffee, before she told him about her job.

"But I don't understand, Margaret. Why?"

"There has to be something more to life than this, Harry."

"I've tried to give you everything you wanted, haven't I?"

"Yes, but..."

"I've spent the last twenty-five years trying to make you happy." Harry slowly stirred his coffee and raised the cup to his trembling lips, and then put it down again. "Look at all the gadgets I've bought you for the kitchen. Even a car of your own."

"Listen, Harry, please just *listen* to me, for God's sake. I need more than gadgets. I need to use my brain."

"What about volunteer work? The Girl Guides are always short of leaders." He picked up his cup and raised it to his lips again. "Look at Fuller's wife; she rolls bandages or something for the cancer people and helps part-time mending books in the library. Sometimes, according to Fuller, they even have her reading to the little ones. You could make yourself useful like that, couldn't you?"

"I like what I'm doing. I get paid, too." She couldn't help slipping that in, but regretted it a moment later as Harry's face went a mottled red. *It's funny how fair-skinned men show their emotions so easily*, she thought.

"Are you trying to tell me I don't provide for you adequately?"

Margaret looked at him sitting in his chair, complete bewilderment on his face. He *really* couldn't see what was wrong with their life. *My God, we are so polite with each other. We can't even have a real mud-slinging, loud row. Even our sex life has become polite.* For a brief moment she felt sorry for him, but that was snuffed when he said, "What will they say at the firm? And they're bound to find out that my wife... of all people, my wife," he spluttered, "is working in a sleazy rundown detective agency."

"Actually, Harry," she said, as she scooped up the cups from the coffee table, "I don't give a damn! And neither should you!" And she marched out the door. In the kitchen, she took a few deep breaths before she began putting the dishes away on the shelves, banging a few cupboard doors for good measure. *And I'm sure as hell not going to give up my job!*

CHAPTER SIX

Sixteen-year-old Sally Fielding desperately wanted her mother. But even more than that, she wanted the awful pain to stop. She buried her face in the pillow to muffle her cries as the next wave of pain wracked her body, but the stern-faced nurse appeared at her bedside anyway.

"Enough of that," she said as she leaned over Sally to prod her swollen abdomen with icy fingers. "You're going to need all your strength soon. Are you timing your pains like I told you to?"

"Yes. Every two minutes," Sally answered miserably. "When is it going to be over?"

"Soon, I hope," the nurse said over her shoulder as she walked toward the door, then added for good measure, "Why do I always get the difficult cases?"

But it was several more hours before Sally looked down at her little dark-haired daughter lying across her stomach. She was still attached to her by the umbilical cord, and Sally put out a tentative hand to touch the damp little head. "She's . . . she's beautiful."

"You did well," the doctor said kindly. "Lie still for a little while and we'll soon have you cleaned up."

She watched the delivery room nurse clean the baby's eyes, fasten a bracelet around the little ankle and then wrap her in a pink blanket. And she knew then what was meant by a broken heart, as she listened to the cries of her newborn baby getting fainter and fainter as they carried her away. "I can't give her up . . . I can't." But they had made it quite clear that if they helped her solve her problem, there would be no turning back.

CHAPTER SEVEN

Harry hid behind his newspaper and gave a grudging thank you when Margaret placed his cereal and coffee before him. He folded the paper precisely to the stock exchange section and reached around it for the cup.

As Margaret gathered up her dishes to take to the sink, Harry finished reading, carefully refolded the paper into its original lines and placed it squarely on the table. "My grey pinstripe suit will be ready at the cleaners," he said, putting the stub on the table, "if you think you can spare the time to pick it up."

"I'll get it tomorrow, Harry," she answered, "when I do my Saturday shopping."

"I take it you intend to go on with this nonsense."

"I haven't changed my mind."

He stood up and brushed non-existent crumbs from his jacket. "If you embarrass me in any way, Margaret, I'll . . ."

"How the hell can my having a job embarrass you?"

"What the girls will say, I can't imagine. And . . ." Another awful thought had come into his head, "what if Mother finds out?"

"Barbara told me just the other day that it was time I found something useful to do. As for your mother . . ."

"Don't you dare say anything about my mother," he said, picking up his briefcase, "after all she's done for us." Margaret thought for an awful moment that he was going to cry, but he continued, "You've changed, Margaret. You've changed." He stalked out of the room and she heard the door slam.

It was well into the morning before her depression lifted and she could concentrate on the job of filing. "Mr. Southby, what are we going to do with all these notes on Collins?" she asked. "Do you want me to throw them out?"

"Don't you think it's about time you called me Nat, Maggie? And regarding the files, I've a hunch that we haven't heard the last of him," he answered. "No, we'll keep them just in case."

"These files are a disgrace," Maggie said, slamming another pile onto her desk to be sorted and reorganized. "How you ever manage to find anything beats me."

"Why do you think I hired you?" he said with a laugh.

Margaret found herself grinning as she reached to answer the telephone. "Southby's Investigations."

"John Cuthbertson here. Would Nat be around?"

"A Mr. John Cuthbertson?" she said as she handed the phone to her boss.

"Hi, Cubby. You've got some news for me?"

"I may have seen that missing boat you were asking about."

"Where? In the marina?"

"I think it passed me last night when I was coming in from fishing. It was being towed in by the Coast Guard."

"You think it was the *Seagull*?"

"It was getting dark, but it was blue and white and I caught part of the name Sea-something. It seemed to be in bad shape."

"You may be onto something, Cubby. Where can I get a look at it?"

"Um . . . ," Cubby answered. "Aw, what the heck, it's Friday. Can you make it to the marina by two?"

"Sure can. Thanks, Cubby."

"Don't bury that Collins file too deep," he said, turning to Maggie. "My friend Cubby thinks he saw the *Seagull* being towed in last night. He's taking me to see it."

"Did he say whether Collins' brother-in-law was on it?"

He shrugged. "Didn't sound like it. He said the boat was badly smashed up. Want to come along?"

"I'd love to, but..."

"Got something more exciting to do?"

Maggie thought about the previous night. "No, not really."

"Then come on. We won't be back late."

"But," Maggie said sweetly, "I thought you were off the case."

He winked at her. "I am, officially. So you're coming?"

Maggie thought for a minute. "Yes."

"Great!" he exclaimed. "Let's go. I'm starved. I'll buy you a hamburger on the way."

CUBBY'S BOAT, SLEEK AND FAST, didn't offer Maggie, sitting on the long seat in the stern, much protection from the cold wind that was blowing down Howe Sound and churning up whitecaps. Cubby had offered her the protection of the cabin, but she had declined, opting instead for fresh air and being able to see where they were going. But although it was a sunny day, she had to snuggle down inside her coat and hope to God she wouldn't lose the lunch that her boss had treated her to. He, on the other hand, sitting next to Cubby in the console, was protected by the windscreen.

"Be there in half a minute," Cubby yelled back to her over the noise of the powerful engines. "Just beyond that point. See?"

Maggie stood up and poked her head, turtle-fashion, out of her collar to peer between the two men through the spray-speckled windshield. She could see that they had rounded a spit and were entering a sheltered bay.

"Coast Guard's over there," Cubby shouted, pointing to a long, low building with the flags of Canada and British Columbia flapping on the foreshore.

"Can we get up close?" Nat Southby shouted.

"I'll try." Cubby nosed the craft right up beside the battered hulk and cut the engine. The detective reached over and grabbed *Seagull's* gunwale. "Jesus Murphy! What a mess!"

Cubby nodded. "It looks as if it was either rammed or smashed up onto some hefty rocks."

"Probably the rocks," Nat said. "There was one helluva storm the night she went missing."

"I can't imagine anyone surviving that," Maggie shuddered. "Are we trespassing, Nat?" she added, unconsciously using his first name.

"Why?"

"There's a man waving his arms at us."

"Let's go, Cubby. I've seen enough." Nat pushed them away from *Seagull*, and Cubby revved the engine.

"Should we see what he wants?" Maggie asked. "He doesn't look very happy."

"I don't think we'll hang around to find out," Nat grinned at her. "Full steam ahead, Cubby."

Nat was the first out of the boat when they arrived back at the marina. Immediately, he put his hand out to help the shivering Maggie over the side. "This coat wasn't meant for the open sea," she said, taking his hand.

"Come on, you two," Cubby said, jumping off the yacht behind them. "I'll treat you both to a hot toddy. Follow me."

Once inside the marina's dining room, her cold hands wrapped around a steaming mug, Maggie began to take an interest in her surroundings. The floor-to-ceiling windows that overlooked the marina gave a clear view across the strait to Vancouver Island.

The cheerful room, warmed by a log fire in a huge stone fireplace, the snatches of conversations going on around her about boats, trips, where the fish were biting or not biting and, of course, the weather, made her realize what a wonderful, different life these people seemed to be enjoying compared to—up to now—her own.

"I see you're back."

Maggie looked up to see a man, stained briar pipe clenched between yellowed teeth, black curly hair escaping from under a greasy, peaked cap, and with the most startlingly green eyes she had ever seen.

"McNab! Here, take a seat," Nat answered, pulling out a chair.

McNab settled in the chair, signalled to the waiter, and then looked pointedly over at Maggie.

"Oh, Maggie, I'd like you to meet Mr. McNab. He's the caretaker of the marina here."

McNab bounced up again and solemnly shook hands with her. "You heard the Collins boat has turned up?" he said, turning to Nat.

"Yes," Nat answered. "Heard it was towed in."

McNab took the glass of Scotch from the waiter. "Here's to ye, laddie," he said, taking a good swig. "That chappie from the Coast Guard came in again this morning, too."

"What did he want?"

"Asking more stupid questions. About you, matter of fact."

"Me? What kind of questions?"

"Wanted to know if I knew ye and why the interest in the *Seagull*." He tossed the remaining Scotch down his throat. "I kinda upset the chappie, told him to get in touch with ye hisself."

"Thanks a lot," Nat said with a grin.

THAT EVENING, MARGARET WAS putting the last touches to the salad when she heard Harry's key in the lock. Determined to be as pleasant as possible, she called out, "Hi, how did your day go?"

"Okay, I suppose." He picked up the evening paper and carried it into the living room.

Margaret, feeling invigorated by her own day's activities, picked up the tray containing Harry's usual Scotch and soda and a sherry for herself, and followed him into the warmth of the living room, where the fire cast flickering shadows on the wall.

Harry took an appreciative swallow of his Scotch. "What's for dinner?"

"Curried chicken. It won't be ready for awhile, so relax and enjoy your drink."

He settled back in his chair and closed his eyes. "I have to go back East again next week," he said abruptly.

"Oh, that's too bad. Can't you send someone else?"

"No. You know I've worked on the Harris case from the beginning."

"When are you leaving, then?"

"Tuesday morning." He took another swallow of his drink. "Margaret..."

"Yes, Harry?"

"Margaret, why don't you come with me?"

"I can't. Not now."

"I don't see why not." He stared moodily into the fire.

"I'm not going through this discussion again, Harry."

"But Margaret, what about me?"

"What about you?"

"This ridiculous job of yours. It's getting in the way of everything."

"Be honest, Harry. How does it really affect you?"

"It stops you coming away with me. That's how it affects me."

"Harry," she said softly, "this is the first time that you've ever asked me to go with you." She got up quietly and left the room.

CHAPTER EIGHT

"Well, Mrs. Spencer, how did your weekend go?" Nat Southby asked as he cruised through the office door, throwing his hat in the general direction of the coat tree.

Bending down to retrieve the hat, Maggie thought of the rotten two days she'd spent with her very stone-faced husband. "Can't say anything exciting happened."

"Is anything the matter?"

"If you can call a husband who doesn't want me to work the mat..."

His face dropped. "You mean here? He doesn't want you to work here?"

"Anywhere."

"You're not going to quit, I hope?"

She stared at her typewriter for a moment. "No," she replied, picking up a piece of paper and rolling it into the machine. "Like it or not, Mr. Southby, I'm here to stay." She gave him a lopsided grin. "And when are you going to get this office an electric typewriter?"

"Good God, woman, you had me worried there for a bit." He touched her lightly on the shoulder as he passed on his way to his office. "As to the electric typewriter, we'll get that when you've proved your worth," he said, and ducked as an eraser came flying toward him.

She was on her hands and knees, sorting piles of papers, when the outer door opened to admit an unsmiling Mark Farthing, accompanied by his carbon copy. Both men were dressed in beige trench coats, black shoes and socks, and sported five-dollar haircuts.

Farthing gave her a curt nod. "Mrs. Spencer, my partner, Constable Stan Haddock. Southby in?"

She clambered to her feet, pulling her skirt down to cover her knees. "I'll tell him you're here."

"Don't bother." He walked over to Nat's door, rapped and opened it.

"Well, if it's not Sergeant Farthing and friend," she heard Nat say. "What can I do for you boys?"

The two men entered the room and closed the door.

"I understand you were hired by a man named Phillip Collins recently?" Farthing asked, taking the only available chair.

"He'd lost a boat."

"Find it?"

"Come off it, Mark. You know as well as I do that it's been found smashed up." Nat watched in exasperation as Haddock, finding nowhere to sit, entertained himself by picking things up from the desk, looking at them and putting them down again. "I'll get Maggie to bring you a chair."

"No, I'm fine." Haddock walked to the window and peered between the slats of the Venetian blinds.

"Anyway, Mark," Nat said, "what's it to you? You're on homicide detail, not lost and found."

"How far did you get with your investigation?"

"Not far." Nat leaned forward to stub out a cigarette in his overflowing ashtray. "Given up cigars," he said with a grin.

Haddock stopped fiddling with the blind and faced Nat. "What do you mean, not far?"

"Got taken off the case."

"Why?" Farthing fished in his coat pocket, pulled out a small notebook and flipped it open.

"Collins decided his wife's brother had taken it and gone on a spree. Paid me and called off the investigation."

Farthing gave an exasperated look at his partner, who was trying to get the wrapper off a stick of gum. "We know you were ferreting around down at the marina," he said. "What did you find out?"

Haddock, having won the battle with the wrapper, had now turned his attention to the foil. "Did you hear anything about the two of them having a set-to?" he said as he rolled the foil into a ball.

Nat watched Haddock in fascination as he slowly folded the gum into his mouth. "Yeah, but my source said he was too far away to know what it was all about." He turned at Mark Farthing. "What gives, Mark? There's more to this than a smashed-up boat, isn't there?"

"Larry Longhurst seems to be missing."

"But how does homicide get into this? You did say missing, not murdered."

Farthing looked down at his notebook. "I hear you were looking over Collins' boat yourself on Friday."

"We tried to, but we were warned off."

"You sure there's nothing else to tell us?"

Nat shook his head. "Like I said, I was taken off the case."

"And you believed Collins' explanation?"

"Why not?" Nat said. "It made sense."

Farthing got up from his chair and gave a nod to Haddock. "That's all for the present. As I said before, Southby, this is police business and I want it to stay that way." He opened the office door. "You do understand?"

"I look after my business," Nat said. "You look after yours." He followed them into the outer office.

"Maybe you should stick to divorce cases, Southby. Oh, wait, I forgot, being on the take is more your style, isn't it?" Farthing said, dripping sarcasm. "By the way, how is your ex? Haven't seen her around town lately," he added as a parting shot.

"On the take? What the hell are you talking about, Farthing?" Nat demanded. "Come back here, dammit!"

"You forget, Southby," Farthing replied with a smirk as he grabbed the handle of the outer door. "I not only took over your desk when you left, but I got all its contents too."

"What the hell are you talking about . . . ?" Nat yelled. But the two men had exited smartly and were by now clattering down the stairs.

"What in heavens name was that all about?" Maggie asked in a shocked voice.

"Beats me," he answered. "I haven't a clue what he meant."

"Why did he come in the first place?" she asked.

"A fishing expedition, Maggie. Just ferreting. Knew I'd been to look at Collins' boat," he answered. "Hoped I'd let something slip, I suppose."

MAGGIE WAS HALFWAY HOME that afternoon when she changed her mind, turned the car around and drove back to Violet Larkfield's house. Parking the car, she walked up the path and rang the bell. The front door was opened abruptly by Violet.

"You again!" she said, looking down at Maggie. "What do you want this time?"

"Uh . . . I wondered how Ernie's cat was." It seemed such a lame excuse that she was sure the woman would see through it.

"A lot better than if she'd stayed with that old man." She started to close the door.

Maggie thought quickly. "Could I see her?"

"What for? I told you she's okay."

"It's just that . . . I like her . . . and cats . . ." she finished lamely. "I sort of feel sorry for her."

A thin smile appeared on the woman's lips, and to Maggie's surprise, she said, "Is that so? Well then, I suppose you can come in."

The smell of cat still permeated the house and Maggie was sure it was the same Siamese that had previously attacked her sitting on the top perch, watching her every move.

"I'll try to find Emily for you. You can sit down." Violet Larkfield indicated the cretonne-covered sofa. "She prefers the outdoors."

Maggie realized that she had only a short time before Violet would be back. But what to look for? How to start? The desk under the window seemed a good place. She looked nervously up at the cats, all seated on their perches and staring silently at her with their green and amber eyes. The desk had several drawers, all locked, of course. Quickly, she flicked through a pile of letters and papers on the desktop. Nothing unusual, mostly bills. She was turning away from the desk when she saw an open film envelope. Picking it up, she tipped the contents out onto the desk and scanned the photos. One of the snaps showed Phillip Collins and his wife standing beside the silver Jaguar. Maggie heard the sound of a door banging, and she reached for her handbag from the sofa and slipped the photo into it. Then, willing herself not to panic, she stuffed the rest of the photos back into the envelope and sat down, just before Violet, with Emily in her arms, came back into the room.

"Here," she said, dumping the cat into Maggie's lap.

The animal struggled to get away. "Nice pussy," Maggie forced out, gamely holding on to the cat and stroking the fur furiously. But Emily had other ideas. "Damn you!" Maggie yelled suddenly as she felt the sharp claws digging into her leg. Emily gave her a disdainful look, swished her tail, jumped down onto the floor and stalked, with dignity, out of the room.

Maggie lifted her skirt and looked at the blood running down her leg. "Vicious little beast!"

"Well," laughed Violet, "I thought you liked cats."

Maggie, needing a Kleenex to clean the blood off her ruined stockings, looked around for her handbag.

"Funny," the sarcastic voice carried on, "first my Satan attacked you and now Emily. Cats know. People you can fool. Cats—never. And if you're looking for your purse, you left it on my desk. Now get out!"

MAGGIE WAS MAKING coffee the next morning when Nat came in. She handed him the picture as he went past on his way to his office. A moment later he was back. "Where'd you get this, Maggie?"

"From Violet. I went to see her yesterday afternoon." She sat and pulled the cover off the typewriter.

"Maggie," Nat said with a worried look, "as you yourself reminded me, I hired you to be a secretary, not an operative."

She took her hands off the keys and stared at him in disbelief. "You didn't mind sending me off on errands last week!" she said haughtily.

"Well, that was different. That was just to take the cat back..."

Maggie was silent.

"What in hell did you think you'd find out?"

"When you've calmed down, *Mister* Southby, maybe I'll tell you."

Nat groaned. "All right, Maggie, I'm calm now. Honest. So you'd better tell me everything from the beginning."

"I was at her desk, you see. And there was this photograph of Collins," she added excitedly. "Everything was going quite well,"

Maggie looked up to see how he was taking her explanation, "until Violet came back in the room before I could look any further..."

"Didn't you realize the risk you were taking? Did she see you at her desk?"

"No, no, she couldn't have. She came in and dumped the cat on my lap, and then the little beast dug its claws into me. But I was right," she ended triumphantly. "There is a connection between Collins and Violet."

He studied the snapshot more closely. "And what happens when she finds it's gone?" he asked.

"She'll think she's mislaid it, I hope."

"So do I, for your sake." Photo in hand, he walked toward his office. "I hate to dash your great detective instincts," he said over his shoulder, "but you know, Maggie," he waved the snapshot at her, "this doesn't prove a thing."

"Of course it does. We've been looking for Collins' boat, his brother-in-law's missing, Violet's related to him in some way and..." she paused for breath, "and she's somehow connected to Ernie's death, too."

"Oh come on, Maggie, that's pushing it. How can you connect her to his death?"

"Ernie knew where to look for his cat when it went missing. And he must have been out looking for the damn thing when he was killed." She sat silent for a moment. "He was just in the wrong place at the wrong time."

THE REGISTERED LETTER DEMANDING Margaret Spencer's attendance at the coroner's inquest into Ernie Bradshaw's death happened to arrive at the Spencer household at the same moment that Harry, concerned that he had a cold coming on, had arrived home for lunch. Since he had to sign for the letter, he felt it was his right to open it.

Margaret arrived home a short while later to be met by an angry and ashen-faced Harry.

"This came for you," he said stonily, handing the envelope over to her.

"You've opened it!"

"Anything that concerns you concerns me, Margaret."

"But you had no right to open my mail," Margaret said furiously.

Harry pursed his lips. "I saw the official address on it. And besides, I signed for it."

"Meaning, I suppose, that you're the only one important enough to receive official letters?"

"That is beside the point, Margaret." He took the envelope out of her hands and opened it again. "It says here," and he pointed to a line in the document, "that you are being summoned to attend an inquest on the murder of somebody called Ernest Bradshaw on Thursday, April 2. I want to know who this man is . . . uh . . . was?"

"He was a client of the agency."

"But why do you have to attend? You're not the detective or whatever it is he calls himself."

"It's quite simple, Harry. We discovered the body together."

"You what?" Harry exploded.

"I was on the case," Margaret answered, trying her best not to smile.

"And you didn't tell me?"

"Why would I tell you? You've made it very clear you're not interested in my job."

"Your job! What kind of man takes you to places where there are dead bodies?"

"Oh, Harry, be reasonable. How would he know that the man was dead when we went to the house?"

"You had no right to be traipsing around town with a strange man."

"Strange? I work for him, for God's sake."

Harry looked shocked. "You never used to swear."

"I'll be swearing a lot more if you keep this up."

"Well," Harry said in his important voice, "it's too late for me to try to fix things."

"Fix things! What are you talking about?"

"If I'd known this inquest was coming up, I'd have fixed it so you wouldn't have to appear."

"Harry," she replied quietly, "you are a corporate lawyer, not a criminal one. You couldn't have fixed it even if I'd wanted you to."

"Let me remind you that I've a good standing in this community," he shot back at her. "There are ways to do these things."

"I've news for you, Harry," she said, taking the letter back from him. "I found the body and I'm going to the inquest."

THE NEXT MORNING, Nat called Maggie into his office. "Listen to this," he said, and began reading from the newspaper spread over his desk.

> The body of a young girl was discovered washed up on Tumbo Island yesterday by a party of birdwatchers. The identity of the young woman has not been released pending notification of next of kin. According to eyewitnesses, the girl appeared to be in advanced pregnancy. When found, she was wearing a life jacket with the name *Seagull* printed on it. Cause of death has not been disclosed by the RCMP officer in charge of the case.

"What about Larry Longhurst?" Maggie exclaimed. "Is he still missing?"

"So far as I know. But what was a pregnant girl doing in Collins' boat?" Nat mused.

"Perhaps Mark Farthing will let something slip," Maggie said. "He's bound to be at the inquest."

"My God! The inquest," Nat said, jumping up. "We're going to be late."

To Maggie's surprise, it was over very quickly. Once again Maggie and Nat were taken step-by-step through their discovery of the body, told to make themselves available for further questioning by the police, and were allowed to leave. The enquiry was adjourned for an additional four weeks, pending further investigation. And Farthing was nowhere in sight when they finally emerged from the building.

"THAT SHOULD BE the end of that," Harry said that evening, when Margaret finished explaining what had happened. "Bradshaw must have disturbed a bunch of young toughs. Nobody's safe these days."

Margaret, knowing that it wasn't the end of it at all, just nodded. Keep the peace. After all, Harry would be off on his trip in a few days.

ALTHOUGH THE RAIN WAS HEAVY the day after Harry's departure for Toronto, Maggie found herself once again, without quite knowing why, turning onto Larch Street on her way home from work. Nearing Violet's house, she spotted a girl who was struggling to open the Larkfield gate, and she pulled over to the side of the road to watch her. The girl put down the overnight case she was carrying so that she could use both hands. Once she had the gate open, Maggie noticed that she seemed to have difficulty bending down to retrieve the case. It was then she realized that the girl was very pregnant. The front door opened abruptly to the girl's knock, and the last Maggie saw of her was Violet yanking her inside.

"Curious," Maggie said aloud as she slipped the car into gear again.

Thoughts in tumult, she reached home and put the car in the garage. "A coincidence?" she asked herself. "Pregnant girl in Collins' boat and another visiting Violet?" She made herself a sandwich and considered calling Nat, but decided to wait until the morning.

But the next morning, before she had time to tell him about Violet's young visitor, he was bursting to tell her his own bit of news.

"Thought you'd like to know that Farthing dropped by to see me after you'd left yesterday," he said.

"Have they found Larry?"

"Didn't say. He wanted me to rehash our finding Ernie."

"Again?"

"Yeah, but he's finally ready to admit I was right about the old man being killed elsewhere."

Her mind went back to that awful scene—broken dishes, upturned furniture and amid the mess, old Ernie, his head bashed in and a bloody crowbar beside him. "What reason did he give?"

"Same as me. Not enough blood," Nat answered her.

"But he was covered in it."

"Yes, but there was none on the walls, floor or furniture," he explained. "If he'd been killed there, the blood would have been spattered everywhere."

"Then what killed him?"

"The iron bar. They put it beside him to make it look as if he'd been killed there."

"Poor man," she said, feeling slightly sick. "Nobody deserves to die like that."

"It happens," Nat replied. "You busy this afternoon?"

"Not particularly," Maggie answered cautiously. "Why?"

"Want to do a bit of sleuthing?"

"Sleuthing? But you said you only hired me for office work."

"I was mad at you for taking things in your own hands," he said apologetically. "You could've been hurt."

Maggie thought for a moment. "Where are you going sleuthing?"

"In Ernie's neighbourhood. Thought you'd like to come along."

"I don't know, Nat, I don't think Ha . . ."

"If we leave right after twelve o'clock," he interrupted her, "you'd be home way before suppertime."

"Well, okay. If you're sure I won't be late back."

Nat smiled as he made his way into his own office.

It was still raining when the two of them climbed into Nat's old Chevy, and when they reached Ernie's house, the overcast skies gave the place the appearance of being even more drab and neglected. "Where do we start?" she asked, reaching for her umbrella.

"With the neighbours on either side of the house. You take the left side."

"On my own? I wouldn't know what questions to ask."

"Just keep it simple, Maggie. Did they hear anything unusual? Did they see any strange cars around? Did they like him? Use your common sense."

"For heaven's sake, what difference does it make if they liked him or not?" she said as she struggled to get a notepad and pencil out of her handbag.

"You'd be surprised the things people notice, particularly if it's someone they dislike," Nat replied as he got out of the car.

"Wouldn't it be better if we did this together?"

"Nope. I'm giving you the opportunity to get your feet wet as an investigator." He strode off.

It took her quite a few minutes to pluck up courage to knock on the first door.

"Yes?" The woman opened the door a crack. Behind her. a small child clung to her skirt. The cloying smell of wet diapers and the shrill wailing of a baby wafted out of the house.

"I would like to ask a few questions . . . about your neighbour," she started, tentatively. "Mr. Bradshaw?"

"He's dead," the woman answered shortly.

"That's what I would like to ask you about."

"Police've been here already. You another one of them reporters?" She started to close the door.

"No. I'm not a reporter," Maggie assured her quickly. "Insurance company," she said, keeping her fingers crossed that the woman wouldn't ask for her credentials. "Did you happen to hear or see anything unusual that night?"

"Didn't think he'd have anything worth insuring."

"You'd be surprised," Maggie answered. "Did you hear anything?"

"Can't say I did. Miserable old bugger."

"Can you remember when you saw him last?"

"Day he was killed. Looking for that blasted cat of his. Bloody thing was always digging up my husband's garden."

Maggie had to shout the next question over the mounting screams of the baby. "Any loud noises that night?"

"No," she yelled back. "Like I told the cops. We didn't hear nothin'." And picking the toddler up, she slammed the door.

"Any luck?" Nat asked when she reached the car.

"No. And she didn't love him either," she said with a grin. "What about you?"

"Nothing. But they did mention the fact that there's a back alley to these places." He buttoned his coat against a sudden gust of wind. "Let's go and see."

As they walked toward the back of the house, Maggie couldn't help but remember their last visit there, with Emily leading the way. Now she followed Nat down the path to a wooden garage or shed that loomed at the end of the yard.

"It obviously backs onto the alleyway," he muttered as they approached the broken-down building and pushed open the door. He took a flashlight from his overcoat pocket and shone it over several old tires, a rusty bicycle hanging from the ceiling, and in one corner, a push-type lawn mower. The large open doors that banged dejectedly in the wind opened onto the alleyway. "Easy to see where they got in," he said.

"But they would have had to carry him, and how did they get from here into the house? There weren't any broken windows."

"Took the keys out of Ernie's pocket, I suppose. I guess the old fool strayed where he shouldn't have."

"Do you realize what this means?"

"No, not really." Nat looked at her, puzzled.

"They, whoever they were," she said slowly, "knew exactly where Ernie lived."

"My God, Maggie, you'll be a detective yet." He linked his arm in hers as they turned away from the garage. "Come on, let's get out of this miserable weather."

"You know, Nat, nobody really cared for the old man," Maggie exclaimed as she settled herself in the car.

"True," Nat answered, "even his cat kept leaving him." He started the car and pulled away from the curb. "Hey, cheer up, Mrs. Spencer," he said. "Let's go and get a bite of lunch."

"No, I think I'd better get back," she answered. "Harry might call from Toronto."

"So what? He can always call back. Do you like Italian?"

"Yes, but . . ."

"That's settled then."

The afternoon passed swiftly and pleasantly. They talked over spaghetti and green salad as if they had known each other for months, not weeks. And to Maggie's surprise, she found that Nat shared her love of classical music. A long time later, she looked reluctantly at her watch. "It's four o'clock, Nat. I don't know where the time's gone."

He nodded, beckoned to the waiter for the bill and then helped her on with her coat. "You can tell Harry from me that he's a very lucky man."

"That's kind. Thank you," she replied with a wry smile.

Back at home, Maggie took one look at the house and realized that she had better clean it up before Harry returned. By six o'clock, she stopped working and made herself a quick sandwich, which she ate while watching the news on the television set. But her mind kept slipping back to the afternoon. *Stop, Maggie*, she scolded herself. *It was only a business lunch.* Tired after the full day, she went to bed early, but as she was reaching to put out the light, the phone rang.

"Is that you, Margaret? Where have you been? I've been trying to get you all afternoon."

"I went out for lunch, Harry."

"Oh!"

"Is anything the matter?"

"Yes. I can't get home until Monday."

"That's too bad. But don't fret about it. Do you want me to meet you at the airport?"

"No, I'll have to go straight to the office. I'll get a cab."

"Fine, Harry. See you Monday night, then." She replaced the receiver and snuggled down in bed, smiling at the prospect of a weekend of peace.

A LITTLE APPREHENSIVE of what to expect, Maggie made sure to arrive at the office before her employer. She needn't have worried.

He just gave her one of his huge grins as he waltzed in, threw his hat at the stand and, missing it as usual, headed into his own office.

"Nat," she said, leaning on the doorpost, his hat in her hand. "What made you go back to Ernie's yesterday? Was it just Farthing's visit?"

"Partly. But the real reason was this." And he handed a cheque to her.

"What's this for?"

"It's a retainer from Bradshaw's lawyer."

"But why? How is he involved?"

"Apparently, Bradshaw's daughter wants me to look into the murder. She doesn't like the way the cops are handling it."

"That's quite a sum. She must have no shortage of money." Maggie handed the cheque back to him.

"So did the old man, from what her lawyer told me."

"How did she hear about you?"

"Maybe Ernie had told her about the number of times I found that wretched cat for him."

"So. What do we do now?"

Nat smiled at the *we*. "We, Maggie old girl, have to get that damn cat back."

"Get it back! From Violet?" She looked at Nat in disbelief. "Oh, no," she said as it dawned on her who would be the getter. "Not me. I'm not going back there. Just let it stay with Violet. It's very happy there."

"Ernie's daughter is the rightful owner, and it's our job to get it back for her."

"Have you called Violet?"

"No, my dear. I was waiting for you!"

CHAPTER NINE

The day after her baby was born, Sally Fielding was sent back to the farmhouse annex. Exhausted from the birth and still crying, she could put up very little fight when the nurse jabbed a needle into her hip and oblivion took over. She awoke to find Debbie gently sponging her face and realized that she was back in the attic bedroom they had shared before her baby's birth. As she felt the warm, hard swelling of Debbie's stomach brush against her, she had a fierce longing for her own baby. She buried her face into the pillow as the hot tears started to run down her cheeks again. "I've got to find out where they've taken my baby."

"How? We don't even know where we are."

"*Rosedale Farm, Linton Road.*"

"How did you find that out?"

"I was in labour for a long time, Debbie," Sally answered, "and they got careless. I managed to walk down the passageway to the nursing station before they found me."

"So?"

"It was on the desk, a letter headed *Rosedale Farm, Linton Road*. It's on Bainbridge Island, in Washington State."

"We're on an island?" Debbie stood up. "I thought we were someplace near Seattle."

"I don't think we're far from it," Sally answered. "I was brought here by car, but it was very late at night. I've no idea which direction we took after Seattle, but I do remember taking a small ferry."

"Just knowing where we are is not going to get your baby back, Sally."

"I'm going to find out who's bought her," Sally cried fiercely, "and I'll make them give her back." She turned to look at Debbie. "That's what they're doing, Deb. They're selling our babies."

"So? You know what that woman said," Debbie said quietly. "If we make a fuss, we won't be allowed to go home."

Sally lifted herself up on her elbow and looked intently at her friend. "What makes you think they'll ever let us go? They're making a fortune out of selling our babies. And we could talk. We're a danger to them."

They were both silent for a moment, then Sally said, "Deb, we've got to get away from here." She clung to her friend's arm.

"You must." Debbie sat down on the edge of the bed. "How can I . . . like this?" She patted her stomach.

"I'll find a way . . . I'll get to a telephone . . . or something."

SERGEANT BRIAN TODD of the Missing Persons Branch closed the file drawer with a bang, walked to the window and stood staring down at the busy street below.

"What's up?" Staff Sergeant George Sawasky asked as he entered the office.

"It's this rash of missing girls," Todd answered him. "Five within the last three months."

"Prostitutes?" Sawasky asked, straddling the wooden chair beside Todd's desk.

"No." Todd walked back to his desk and picked up a file. "That's what's odd about it. Most of them are high school students."

"Any pattern emerging?" Sawasky asked. "The reason I'm

asking," he continued, "is that I'm looking into the death of a teenager, too. A Jane Doe."

"Well, these are all teenagers," Todd answered. "Take this one, Sally Fielding—sixteen years old, good family, and up to five months ago, an A student."

"What happened five months ago?"

"The Fieldings say she just became a changed girl. Depressed, irritable. Grades fell off and they couldn't get her to talk to them."

"All teenagers go through that stage, Brian," Sawasky answered, taking the file to examine the photos the family had provided.

"I said as much to the parents, but they said it had to be something more. It was too much of a change too quickly."

"Drugs?"

"They don't think so." Todd walked over to his filing cabinet and picked out another folder. "And look at this one—Debbie Shorthouse. Seventeen, still in school when she went missing."

"What are the parents like?" Sawasky took the file from him.

"Professional couple, father an electrical engineer, mother a nurse at Vancouver General. Just days prior to the girl's disappearance, they'd found out she was pregnant."

"Pregnant?" Sawasky stared hard at the face of the girl in the photo.

"That your Jane Doe?"

Sawasky shook his head. "No. Mine's blonder than this one." He closed the file and handed it back. "How'd the parents react?"

"Not too pleased." Todd continued. "Father did the old 'how dare you sully my good name' routine. Mother suggested an abortion or a prolonged visit to a distant aunt back east, but the girl absolutely refused and told them she could look after herself. She disappeared less than a week later."

"What about the others?"

"There's a June Cosgrove, went to the same school as Sally Fielding." He handed the Cosgrove file to Sawasky.

"Was she pregnant, too?"

"If the parents knew, they didn't tell me." He began fishing out another file.

"Hold it," Sawasky said. "I think this may be my Jane Doe."

"Where was she found?"

"Washed up on one of the Gulf Islands a couple of weeks ago."

"Oh yeah... something about a stolen boat, wasn't it?"

"That's right," Sawasky answered. "The *Seagull*. We actually found the boat about a week before the body turned up."

"What's the connection?"

"She was wearing a life jacket from the *Seagull*."

"Hard to identify after a week in the sea." Todd gave an exaggerated shudder.

"It's not my idea of fun."

"You find the owner of the boat?"

"A guy named Collins. He maintains that his wife's young brother took it. Says he's going to kill him." He grinned. "We're hoping to find him first."

"The body still in the morgue?"

"Yeah," Sawasky said, reaching for his coat. "You wanna go down?" He tucked the Cosgrove file under his arm.

A short while later, the two officers were looking with revulsion on the remains of the fair-haired girl. "My God!" Todd muttered and turned away.

"You think that could be the Cosgrove girl?" Sawasky asked, passing the file over. "Looks about the right age to me."

"Could be," he answered, "but she's too decomposed to be sure." Sawasky picked up the x-ray of the corpse's teeth just as Todd fished the dental records out of the Cosgrove file. They stared from one to the other. "Yeah," Sawasky said and he gave a curt nod to the attendant for him to re-zip the white body bag.

"I'll have to get the parents over to ID her," Todd said, watching as the body was returned to Receptacle No. 30.

ONCE AGAIN, ARMED WITH a brand new wicker basket, Maggie found herself walking up Violet Larkfield's front path. "This is getting to be too much of a habit," she muttered as she steeled herself for another encounter of the worst kind.

"Thought it'd be you," Violet greeted her. "He gets you running all his errands, doesn't he?" Grabbing the basket out of Maggie's arms, she pointed in the direction of the all-too-familiar living room. "You can wait in there. Take awhile to round her up."

Maggie skirted the cat pole that, to her relief, only had a couple of cats on it, neither one the Siamese. She was so concerned with her safety that it was a moment before she saw the man writing at the desk. "Oh, I'm sorry," she said, "I didn't realize anyone was here."

He turned toward her. "Come for that cat, I suppose."

"Yes, I . . . Good heavens, it's Mr. Collins!"

"My aunt said you'd be coming. Take a seat."

"Your aunt?" Maggie asked with surprise.

"Stephanie's aunt, actually." When Maggie looked puzzled, he added, "Steph's my wife."

"Oh, I see. I saw your car here once, but . . . I didn't realize . . ." Her voice trailed off as Collins turned back to the desk. "Have you heard anything more on your brother-in-law?" she asked his back.

Without bothering to face her, he said curtly, "As a matter of fact, I heard yesterday. Sprained wrist, dislocated shoulder and a lot of bruises."

"Where was he all this time?"

"Victoria General. He had a concussion, and it was days before he was able to tell them who he was."

"But it's more than a month since he disappeared!"

"Stayed with a friend after he was discharged. The little shit was scared what I might do to him, I suppose."

"But he must have realized the police would've been looking for him."

Collins shrugged. "He does now."

The sharp voice of Violet Larkfield came from the doorway. "There you go again! Picking on the boy when he's down!" She thrust the basket into Maggie's arms. "Here's the cat, and this'd better be the last time."

"I hope it is too, Mrs. Larkfield," Maggie answered her sweetly. She turned back to Collins. "Goodbye, Mr. Collins, I'm glad . . ."

"Don't keep her in that thing too long," Violet interrupted. "Cats hate to be cooped up." And Maggie once again found herself outside the front door.

By the time Maggie reached the office, Emily was thoroughly fed up with confinement and had set up a constant meowing and pawing at her wicker cage.

"Can't you shut that damn thing up?" Nat said, emerging from his office, looking irritated.

Maggie didn't answer. She just stood there with a wide grin on her face.

"Okay, never mind. Tell me. What happened at Violet's?"

"Phillip Collins! That's what happened."

"Not another fleeting glimpse of a silver car?"

"In the flesh and sitting in Violet's living room. She's his wife's aunt."

"Aunt!" he said slowly. "Maggie, it looks like I owe you an apology."

"You certainly do." She smiled. "And in exchange, I'll give you some more juicy news." She paused dramatically. "Larry has been found—alive and not so well."

"Has he, by God?" He watched as Maggie released the frantic cat from the carrier. "Where was he found?"

"Collins didn't say where exactly. But he's been in the Victoria General, recovering from concussion, a sprained wrist and a dislocated shoulder."

"Sounds as if Collins was quite talkative."

"I might have got more out of him if Violet hadn't come back with the cat. She sure had me out of that front door in a hurry."

"This puts a different slant on things," Nat said thoughtfully. He bent down, gave the cat a tentative pat, and returned to his office.

An hour later, Emily, curled up in a fluffy white ball on the visitor's chair, lazily opened one eye to look at Nat as he came from his office.

"I'm off, Maggie," he said, reaching for his coat. "Got an appointment to set up surveillance for Wong Industries at one."

"But what about Mrs. Read? She's coming in at one to sign the agreement and collect the cat."

"Damn! I forgot." He glanced at his watch. "You don't mind waiting for her, do you?"

"I hope she's on time," Maggie answered. "Harry came home yesterday and I've shopping to do."

"Come on! You know you're curious to see what she looks like," Nat said, and with a wicked grin, he sped through the door.

But it was well after two o'clock before Mrs. Read, a thin, sour-faced woman, opened the door. Her resemblance to Ernie was uncanny.

"It's too hot in here," she complained, sinking into the nearest chair, "and those stairs are a killer."

"Why don't you take your coat off and I'll . . ." Maggie began.

"Haven't time." Dorothy Read fixed her pale grey eyes on Maggie. "Where's that Southby fellow? He's supposed to meet me and go over things."

"There's only this agreement for you to sign at the moment," Maggie answered smoothly, putting it in front of her. "He'll be in touch with you later." She passed a pen over to the woman. "Oh, and we do have your father's cat here for you." She pointed to the basket behind her desk, where Emily now resided quietly.

"I'm not taking that animal!"

"But Mrs. Read, you've got to take her."

"Out of the question! I hate all cats and that one in particular." She set her mouth in a tight line. "Take it to the vets and have it done away with. Put it on my bill. Southby will overcharge me anyway, and a bit more won't matter much."

Maggie opened the basket and revealed Emily daintily washing behind her ears. "You know, she's quite a nice clean cat," she pleaded. "And it seems a shame, when your father was so fond of her."

"That thing hates me. Here, I've signed this." She pushed the paper back across the desk and got up from the chair. "Anyway, it got him killed, didn't it?"

"Why do you say that?"

"He called me that night."

"Did he?"

"He'd been looking for the thing all day and he said he was going out again."

"Can you remember what time he called you?"

"Must've been after six. The old skinflint always waited for the cheap rate time to call me."

"Did he say where he was going to look?" Maggie asked hopefully.

"Said something about going back to where it was found before."

"I see. Did your father carry large sums of money with him, Mrs. Read?"

"You've got to be kidding," she said, starting for the door. "Kept it all in the bank, he did. And look where it got him—dead, with his head bashed in!"

To Maggie's surprise, there was a catch in Dorothy Read's voice. "Mrs. Read," she said, "won't you reconsider taking Emily with you?"

"No. You keep the damn thing if you like it so much." She took a tissue from her pocket and blew her nose. "He wasn't all that bad, you know. You tell that Southby to find out who killed him." And she stamped out the door.

Maggie sat for a few minutes before picking Emily up in her arms. "Well, puss," she said, stroking the soft fur, "it looks as if we're stuck with each other." She eased the squirming cat gently back into the basket. "God knows what Harry is going to say."

"YOU KNOW I'M allergic to cats," Harry sulked.

"Oh, now, Harry, how can you say you're allergic to cats when we've never had one before?"

"Mother always worried about my allergies and she never allowed a cat into the house."

"Your mother . . . ." Margaret stopped herself in time. "It's quite likely you've grown out of those childhood allergies by now."

In the end, Emily somehow sensed her fate was up to her. After dinner, when Harry was dozing in his armchair, she jumped gently onto his lap, turned around three times, blissfully closed her eyes and started to knead his leg. Margaret couldn't help smiling when she came into the room with the coffee to see the two of them dozing by the fire, Harry's fingers gently caressing Emily's ears.

The next day was the beginning of the Easter holiday weekend.

Emily, now feeling one of the family, sat on the wide windowsill and preened herself in the sunshine, eyeing the birds longingly. Harry, pleased to have a few days off, had decided to tidy up the garden, rake leaves and then clean all the garden tools. Margaret was busy cooking, because Midge was coming home for the weekend. Although she tried hard not to show it when Barbara was around, there was a special bond between Midge and herself. The whole family would get together on Easter Sunday, when Barbara and her husband Charles came for dinner.

Let's hope Barbara's not in one of her preachy moods. Her thoughts were suddenly interrupted by the slamming of a car door, and a few minutes later, Midge and a lanky, shaggy-haired young man bounced into the room. Midge was holding onto his arm.

"Mum, this is Jason. Jason, meet my mum—the great detective."

Margaret laughed as she wiped her floury hands on a towel. "So glad to meet you at last, Jason. But a detective I'm not. Just a Girl Friday for one."

"I bet you solve all his cases for him anyway," Midge said as she gave her mother a squeeze.

"I hope it's okay me coming with Midge," Jason said, taking her hand firmly into his. "She insisted you wouldn't mind."

"I told you where I met Jason, didn't I?"

"When you were on duty in the emergency ward, wasn't it?"

Midge nodded. "The stupid dolt had sprained his knee playing football. He's still having a bit of a problem with it, so I couldn't leave him behind now, could I?"

"Certainly not," Margaret said, "as long as he doesn't mind sleeping on the sofa bed in the guest room." At that point Emily decided to let her presence be known, and jumping down from the sill, wound herself through Midge's legs.

"A cat! Mum, you've got a cat!"

"Yes," Harry said as he entered. "Against all my objections."

"But where did it . . . she . . . or whatever come from?"

"Her name is Emily and it's a long story. I'll tell you later," Margaret answered, giving her daughter a warning look.

"Well, she's beautiful," Midge said, scooping Emily up in her arms. The cat rubbed her head under Midge's chin. "Come on, Jason," Midge said, as she reluctantly put the cat down on the floor, "let's get our stuff from the car, and then I'll show you the rest of the house."

"Hold on a minute, Mildred," Harry interrupted. "You haven't said a proper hello to your father yet."

"Mildred?" Jason exclaimed.

Midge laughed, and going over to her father, gave him a hug. "Yes, Jase, that's the name on my birth certificate."

"And a good solid name it is, too," Harry said primly. "It's my mother's second name. But for some obscure reason, my daughter prefers Midge."

"Mildred's a very nice name," Jason said gallantly.

Sunday dinner was quite successful. Margaret thought how nice it was to see the two young couples laughing and talking together. The only sour note was overhearing Barbara and Midge talking as they set the table.

"I hope you've talked to her about her working in that awful place," Barbara said.

"Certainly not," Midge had replied. "I think it's the best thing that ever happened for her."

"But it's humiliating for Father. And it's not as if they need the money."

"For God's sake, Barbara," Midge answered, "this is the fifties! Why shouldn't Mum work if she wants to? Anyway, it's really none of our business."

"But it's not fair to Father! And then she brings that dreadful cat into the house, knowing that Dad and I are allergic to cats."

"Emily and Dad are getting on just fine," Midge answered her. "He just doesn't want to admit it."

Barbara sniffed. "I should have known you'd be on Mum's side."

"Yes, and so should you. Come on, Barbara, don't spoil the weekend."

TUESDAY MORNING BROUGHT Sergeant Farthing and his sidekick Haddock back to Southby's office.

"He in?" Farthing nodded toward the closed door.

"Not yet, Sergeant. Is Mr. Southby expecting you?"

"We won't take up much of his valuable time."

"He is expecting a client."

"*We* expect to be brief, Mrs. Spencer."

Farthing sat staring into space while Haddock did his usual prowl, until Nat finally burst through the door, flinging his hat at the elusive stand. "Hi Maggie, how . . ." He stopped short. "What the hell do you two want?"

"Just a chat." Farthing nodded toward Nat's room. "Shall we?" Nat led the way. "What do you know about Collins and his brother-in-law, Larry Longhurst?" Farthing said without preamble.

"Only what I said before. Why?"

"We've hauled Longhurst in for questioning."

"On what charge?"

"We think he had a passenger."

"Yeah," Nat said. "I read in the paper. Some pregnant girl found wearing a *Seagull* life jacket."

"How about some pooling of ideas?" Farthing suggested.

Nat laughed. "Since when do you need me?" He leaned back into his chair. "You're not getting anywhere with Longhurst, you mean."

"Did Collins ever mention a June Cosgrove?"

"No. Is that the girl in the life jacket?"

Farthing nodded.

"So why come to me?"

"Because I want you to tell your client, from me, that I'm sure as hell they're both lying, and I'm going to get 'em yet." He tipped his head toward Haddock and started for the outer office.

"Hey, before you go," Nat yelled after the departing pair, "what was that crack you made about taking over my old office?"

"All in good time, Southby," Farthing said, tapping the side of his nose with his finger as he pulled violently on the outer door. As he did so, a tall, pale, nervous-looking man practically fell into the room. Bewildered, he shrank back as the two men pushed by him and clattered down the stairs. Maggie, seeing the anxiety on the man's face, managed to get to him before he turned and followed them. Gently, she took his arm.

"Mr. Nielson?"

The man nodded, blinking myopically through his thick lenses.

"Mr. Southby is ready for you." She led him into Nat's room. "This is Mr. Nielson," she said and went out quickly, closing the door behind her.

Nat stood and leaned across his desk to shake Nielson's hand. "You're right on time, Mr. Nielson. Make yourself comfortable. If you'll excuse me for just a moment." And he followed Maggie to the outer office.

"Time to go sleuthing again, Maggie, old girl."

"Where to this time?"

"I want you to find out where a June Cosgrove lived, what school she attended and when the funeral's to be held."

"June Cosgrove? Who's she?"

"The girl that was found drowned on Tumbo Island."

"Where do I start?"

"The story's bound to be in today's *Sun*. Call them."

After Maggie had taken coffee in for Nat and his client, she returned to her desk and reached for the phone. She soon learned that June's funeral would be held the following Thursday, ten o'clock, at Walter's Funeral Chapel in Richmond, that the deceased had attended Richmond High and that her parents lived on Francis Road just off No. 2 Road in Richmond.

"There will be two more mourners on Thursday," Nat said when she gave him all the details after Nielson had left. "There's bound to be a crowd, and nobody will notice us."

"WHY DOES IT ALWAYS rain at funerals?" Maggie asked, as she stepped out of Nat's car into a puddle. "And we're miles from the chapel," she added as she struggled to put up her umbrella. "And I hate funerals!"

"Stop grumbling, woman," Nat said, as he took her elbow and steered her around another muddy puddle.

During the ceremony, Maggie was very moved by the genuine grief of the students from June's school. Afterwards, as the crowd began to disperse, she saw one girl sobbing uncontrollably and being comforted by a boy about the same age. Remembering Nat's suggestion that she should try to talk to some of the girls, she made a sign to him and quickly followed the two teenagers as they crossed the road and entered a small café in the next block.

When she followed them inside and saw them sitting at the counter, she quietly slid onto the empty stool next to the girl. "You must've been very close to June," she said.

The girl turned to face her. "Yes," she answered.

The boy put a protective arm around the girl. "You a reporter or something?" he asked.

"I was at the funeral," she said, evading the question.

"We can't believe she's dead," the girl said, dabbing her eyes.

"Could I get you a Coke, maybe?" Maggie said, touching the girl's shoulder.

"I've already ordered," the boy said brusquely as the waitress set down two Cokes in front of them. "Who are you?"

"Can I get you something?" the waitress asked Maggie.

"Coffee will be fine," she answered, and then turned to the boy. "To answer your question, I'm an investigator." She now had the boy's full attention.

"So whatcha investigating?"

"I was just wondering ... when was the last time you saw June?"

"How do we know you're what you say you are?"

"Cool it, Tom." The girl touched his sleeve. "I haven't seen June since she left school," she said, nervously twisting a silver ring on her index finger.

"How long ago was that?"

The girl thought for a moment. "Must be at least a couple of months."

"You were her friend?"

The girl nodded miserably. "Yes."

"You knew she was going away?"

"You sure you're not a cop?" the boy broke in.

Maggie glanced at the boy. "No," she answered him. "I'm trying to find out what happened."

"I'd like to know what happened, too," the girl said slowly.

"You knew she was pregnant?"

The girl nodded.

"Do you know who the father was?"

"The guy she was going around with. A real jerk."

"Do you think she went away with him?"

"Him? She told me they were through."

The boy stood up. "Come on, Val, we'd better go."

"When did she tell you that?" Maggie laid her hand on the girl's arm. The girl slid off the stool.

"Just before she disappeared. She called me."

"Did she say what she was going to do? Please, Val, this could be very important."

"She said everything was fixed up. She'd met up with someone who was going to help her."

"Did she say who?" Maggie felt a rush of excitement.

"Some guy that used to go to our school. He was going to take her to meet someone. Some kinda private adoption place."

"And that's where she went?"

"I dunno." The girl's voice shook.

"Come on, Val, let's get outta here." The boy pulled her toward him.

"Just a minute," Maggie said, fishing in her bag for a pen. "If you should think of anything else, please call me."

The girl nodded. "Okay, but I don't know anything else."

After Maggie had written her name on the back of one of Nat's cards, she handed it over to the girl. "Anything," she said urgently. "Doesn't matter what."

Outside, Nat was waiting beside his car, and he quickly opened the passenger door. "Thought you were never coming. Everyone has left for the cemetery."

"Do we have to go? I hate intruding on their grief like this."

"It's the only time we'll see so many people who knew her."

On the way, Maggie filled Nat in on her conversation with the two teens in the café. "I didn't learn much, I'm afraid," she concluded.

"On the contrary. Not so bad for an amateur."

By the time they reached the cemetery, the brief service was nearly over. Standing well back, they surveyed the mourners.

The parents were easy to pick out. The woman was sobbing at the graveside with a boy of twelve or so and a young girl, who held onto her mother's coat, looking completely bewildered by the event. Beside them a stern-featured man stared fixedly into the open grave.

"Look, Nat, over there," Maggie said, tugging his arm. "Isn't that Sergeant Farthing?"

"Yep. And I expect Haddock is lurking around somewhere too. Come on, Maggie, let's go before they see us."

CHAPTER TEN

Monday morning the sky was that perfect luminescent blue that May sometimes brings to the British Columbia coast. The air was warm, and the people hurrying to work seemed to be defying the old warning that Maggie's Scottish grandmother used to quote—*ne'er cast a clout 'til May is out*—and were baring their limbs to the gentle breezes.

She hummed to herself as she slipped the key into the door of the office just in time to hear the telephone. "Oh damn," she said as she lunged for the instrument, but the caller had already hung up.

There was a note on her desk from Nat. *Won't be in this morning. Leave messages on my desk. Nat.*

Then this is the perfect day to sort the rest of the files, she thought, and was well into the loathsome task when the phone rang again.

"Mrs. Spencer?"

"Yes."

"It's Val."

"Val?"

"Yeah. You remember, last Thursday at the funeral."

Maggie's mind did a mental flip. "Yes, of course, Val."

"You told me to call."

"You thought of something, then?" she asked encouragingly.

"June told me where she was going to meet that guy that was going to help her."

"Yes?" Maggie wanted to shout at the girl to get on with it.

"It was a restaurant in North Van."

"Do you remember the name of it?" She reached for her notepad and pencil.

"The Blue Plate Café."

"Val, think carefully. Do you remember what day she was going to meet him?"

"March 17th."

"You're sure?"

"Yeah. Saint Patrick's Day. I was getting ready to go to the St. Pat's sock hop at our school when she called."

"Did she say what time?"

"She was leaving right then."

"What time was that?"

"About seven, I guess."

"You've been a great help, Val. Do you have a number where I can call you?"

"Tom wouldn't like it."

"I'd like to let you know how this turns out."

"Well, okay. It's Central 0033."

Maggie replaced the receiver. "Maggie, I think you will be treating yourself to lunch today!"

The Blue Plate Café lived up to its name. Blue drapes, blue walls, blue willow plates on arty, imitation knotty pine shelves. The theme had also been carried into the alcove booth to which she was shown. The elderly blue-gingham-clad waitress poured coffee into a blue cup as she took Maggie's order.

As the Blue Plate special was placed in front of her, Maggie inquired, "You work here long?"

"Since it opened." The waitress, who wore a label saying her name was Pearl, gave a sniff. "Two years come June."

"You like it here, then?"

"It's a job." Pearl topped up Maggie's cup and turned on her heel.

Maggie inspected the clientele. Very few tables were taken, and she could understand why when she sipped the watery vegetable soup. The toasted cheese sandwich was only slightly more appetizing.

"Yer want yer Jell-O?" The blue apparition was back.

"Jell-O? No thanks."

"Goes with the special."

"Do you work in the evenings too?"

"When it's busy."

"I don't suppose you remember if you worked on Saint Patrick's Day?" she asked hopefully.

Pearl rested the coffee jug on the table. "Saint Patrick's Day... Lemme see... yeah... That's the day my Dennis brought home the green shamrock cake. You ever had one of them from Safeway? They're real nice."

"Was it a busy night?"

"Fairly. Why?"

Maggie decided to appeal to the woman's curiosity. "It's rather confidential."

"Yeah?" She bent closer to Maggie.

"I'm trying to find out what happened to a young girl who came in here that night."

It was the right bait. "Let me serve the other table. Then I'm off duty," she said conspiratorially. "I'll be back." Fifteen minutes later, minus blue garb, Pearl slid into the booth opposite Maggie. "Whatcha wanna know?"

"Do you remember seeing a blonde girl, around eighteen or so, come in here with two men that night?"

Pearl shook her head. "Not offhand. What did the guys look like?"

"I don't know for certain, but one of them would have been a fellow around twenty." Maggie paused, considering how to describe Collins. "The other might be in his forties."

The waitress leaned back in the booth and pulled a packet of Players out of her pocket. "This girl, was she pregnant?" she asked, lighting the cigarette and taking a deep draw.

Maggie looked at her in astonishment. "You remember them?"

"Yeah. Though it's the older guy I remember most."

"Do you know his name?"

"Nah. I only remember him because of his creamer castles."

"Creamer castles?"

"Yeah, you know." She reached for the plate of tiny coffee cream tubs beside the ketchup bottle. "Piles these things up, then leaves me the mess to clear up."

"And he's been in several times?"

"Yeah. And I remember him coming in with a girl one other time. Young enough to be his daughter," she said with a sniff.

"You wouldn't be able to pick him out if he came in again, would you?"

"Don't know." The waitress laughed and got up. "Not unless he built another castle."

Maggie scanned her bill, added an extra two dollars to the total and handed it, with one of the agency's business cards, to the waitress. "Please call me if he comes in again, will you, Pearl?"

She was deep in thought as she walked toward her car, so that the touch on her arm made her draw back instantly.

"It is Maggie . . . Nat's Maggie . . . isn't it?"

Maggie looked up at the man who was smiling at her. "I'm sorry, I . . . good heavens, Mr. Cuthbertson."

"Cubby. Do you live in these parts too?"

"No, just shopping over here, so I stopped in for lunch at the Blue Plate." She gave a shudder at the memory of the food. "You said, *too*. Do you live in North Van, then?"

"Most of my life. Got time for another cup of coffee?"

Maggie thought back to the tepid liquid in the café. "Thanks, one was enough," she said, grinning. "And I have to get back."

"Where's your car?"

"Right here." She patted the red Morris. Sliding behind the wheel, she rolled down the window. "Nice seeing you again... Cubby."

"Don't let Nat work you too hard," he said with a grin. He stood at the curb and watched until Maggie's little car disappeared into the traffic. When she reached the office, Nat still hadn't returned. She scribbled a note and left it on his desk on her way out.

WHILE MAGGIE HAD BEEN lunching in North Vancouver, her boss had been having a sandwich with Sergeant Brian Todd of Missing Persons. Their association went back to when Todd had been a hotshot rookie under Nat in the vice squad.

"So what is it you want, Nat?" Todd said, taking a huge bite out of his ham-on-rye. "You haven't taken me out to lunch just because you like my pretty face."

Nat picked up a french fry and dipped it into the ketchup. "I just need a little information."

"About what?"

"Missing teenagers, for a start."

Todd lowered his sandwich. "How did you know?"

"Know what, Brian?" Nat asked innocently.

"About the missing girls?"

"Just a hunch." Nat took a stab at his coleslaw. "How many are there?"

"You know damn well I can't give you that info."

"Just a hint. Are there many similar cases on your files?"

"Similar! What do you mean?"

"For Chrissake, Brian. Same age group, decent homes, bright students and . . ." he paused significantly, "pregnant."

"It looks like you've got inside information already."

"I need names, Brian. Names."

"You know that's confidential."

Nat leaned earnestly toward Todd. "It's not the girls I'm after, but the people who are behind their disappearance. Do you want to have more of them dragged out of the sea?"

"So that's it. You're investigating the *Seagull* case." Todd took another half-hearted bite of his sandwich.

Nat nodded.

Todd forked up the last of his french fries, wiped his mouth on a paper napkin and stood up. "Thanks for lunch." He reached for his jacket. "Look, Nat, we're working with the RCMP on this one. And if Farthing finds out I've been talking to you . . ." He left the sentence unfinished.

"He won't. Come on, Brian. Help me."

Todd hesitated. "You didn't get the names from me."

"What names?" Nat said and signalled to the waiter.

CHAPTER ELEVEN

"And how's your little job going?" Harry asked, taking a sip of brandy. They sat in their usual places on either side of the fireplace.

Margaret looked up in surprise from the newspaper she was reading. "Very well, Harry. How's yours?"

"There's no need to be sarcastic, Margaret."

"You just surprised me."

"I was taking Barbara's advice. That's all."

"And what did Barbara advise you to do, Harry?"

"She said I should show more interest in what you're doing."

"That was nice of her." Margaret lowered the paper to her lap. "When did you speak to her?"

"She called in at the office yesterday." Margaret could always tell when he was hiding something. His face got red and splotchy.

"And she suggested that, if you didn't push me, I would soon tire of *my little job* and give it up, isn't that it?"

"She only remarked that you could be very stubborn. She's quite concerned about you, you know. As am I . . ." Luckily for Harry, the phone rang at that moment. "It's for you," he said. "A man."

"That will be my boss."

"Got your message, Maggie," Nat's voice boomed over the phone. "You should have told me where you were going."

"You weren't there to be told."

"Don't go off on your own again, Maggie," he answered her. "It could be dangerous."

"Now, come on, I only spoke to the waitress, for heaven's sake!"

"Well, okay, now listen, I've got some news too."

"On Sally?"

"No, a list of girls who've disappeared over the past few months."

"How on earth did you manage that?"

"There's ways." He paused for a moment. "Look, Maggie, I think this could become pretty messy. Promise me you won't go off on your own again."

"I'll see you in the morning, Mr. Southby." She smiled as she put the phone down.

"I can't see the necessity of him calling you during the evening," Harry complained.

"You get phone calls out of office hours, Harry."

"That's different. You're only a part-time secretary."

She sat down again in her chair, picked up the newspaper and hid her face behind it. Harry would have been astounded if he had seen the huge grin on her face as she settled down to read.

IN THE OFFICE the next morning, Maggie scanned the list. "These girls are mostly from Richmond or Kitsilano."

"Yeah. Interesting, isn't it? Todd refined the list to middle-class teens with no criminal record, missing in the last two years. And that's what he came up with."

"What do we do now?"

"Check the phone book and match addresses. Then do a little phoning."

"I don't think I could intrude on people like that."

"That's part of the business."

"But what questions do I ask?"

"How long have the girls been missing? Have they heard from them at all? Any reason why they would run away? You'll have to play it by ear."

"Well, okay," she said hesitantly and reached for the phone book.

By the third day, Maggie and Nat between them had located the parents of nine girls who had disappeared under similar circumstances, and she had made up files on each of them, summarizing the information they had gathered. She put the summary on Nat's desk.

Sally Fielding: Age sixteen. Attended Kitsilano High. Missing four months. Father a dentist, mother owns hat shop. Haven't heard from their daughter. Agreed to an interview. June Cosgrove: Age seventeen. Since been found—dead. Has younger brother and sister. Parents devastated. Also went to Kitsilano High. The Cosgroves reluctantly agreed to interview. May Rothstein: Age eighteen. Missing five months. Attending Sprott–Shaw secretarial school at the time she went missing. Parents own two flower shops. Very bitter and will not agree to an interview. The pattern continued down the page: Lucy Childer, Jalna Hunsche, Janice Diebel, Debbie Shorthouse, Olga Koziki. In most cases, the parents agreed to an interview, albeit with not much enthusiasm.

The first break came when Maggie called Amelia Holland's parents. Amelia was seventeen, the parents knew she was pregnant, and she had called them after her disappearance, six weeks ago. She told them that she was someplace near Seattle. She was crying, then just as she was telling them she wanted to come home, the line went dead. The police, when contacted, had said it was impossible to trace the call, and anyway, it was obvious that the girl had gone off to the United States on her own accord. The Hollands readily agreed to an interview.

"Okay," Nat said, looking down the list. "We start on Monday. Set up an interview with the Hollands first."

"Monday's no good for the Hollands," she told him. "He works nine to five, and she teaches night-school cooking classes. They asked if you could come tomorrow morning?"

"No, that's out for me. See if Sunday afternoon is good for them. Around two o'clock," he answered, and picking up the newly-made Holland file, took it into his office. "Oh! What about you, Maggie?" Nat called out to her. "Can you make Sunday afternoon?"

"You don't need me there."

"You know damn well you want to be there. Anyway, I need you to take notes."

"I don't know, Nat. Harry..." Then she remembered the patronizing way Harry had spoken about her job. "On second thought," she said, "I'd love to come."

"Great. Meet me here at one-thirty. We'll take my car."

HARRY LAID DOWN HIS knife and fork. "I've invited Mother over for dinner. It's been such a long time since she was here."

Margaret took a firm grip on herself before answering. "What a good idea. When's she coming?"

"Sunday."

"You mean this Sunday?"

"Of course."

"You could have checked with me first, Harry. How'd you know whether it would be convenient?"

"Convenient! Why shouldn't it be convenient?" Harry patted his mouth with his napkin and resumed eating. "You *are* aware that she hasn't been too well lately?"

"What time are you picking her up?"

"I thought *we* would pick her up about one o'clock. Give us time to drive her around Stanley Park for a change."

Oh, hell! Margaret thought. *Well, here goes.* "I'm afraid it will be just you picking her up, Harry. I have a prior appointment."

"Appointment! What kind of appointment can you possibly have on a Sunday?" Harry glared across the table at her. Then his face reddened as he slammed down his napkin. "I know, I know, it's that blasted job, isn't it?"

"I'll be back in plenty of time to get dinner." She picked up the plates and turned toward the kitchen. "Anyway, Harry, you know your mother would love to have you to herself for an afternoon."

"That's not the point. You're my wife and . . ." But the kitchen door had already swung shut behind her.

Margaret spent Sunday morning preparing a dinner that she could slide into the oven on her return home, and Harry spent his morning shut up in the den with his hi-fi. He played Bach's *Toccata and Fugue in D Minor*—full blast—the organ's crashing notes sending shivers down Margaret's spine as she chopped vegetables for the casserole. *I think he's still a mite mad*, she thought as she floured the cubes of beef, *but they do say music soothes the savage beast, I mean breast.* She was grinning as she browned the meat.

THE HOLLANDS LIVED in a house on West Twelfth. The door was opened before Nat even rang the bell, and Joan Holland led the way into a comfortable living room, its large windows facing Connaught Park.

"It's very good of you to see us," Nat offered, sitting down.

"We'll do anything if it means finding Amy." Joan Holland sat on the arm of her husband's chair. "We just don't know what to do next, do we, Eric?"

Her husband put his hand over hers. "Perhaps there's hope now?" he said.

Nat gave a gentle cough. "I can't promise anything, you realize. Perhaps if you told us what happened from the beginning..."

It was the same story Nat and Maggie had heard in phone calls to other parents: Amelia had been a good student, well liked, belonged to a church group, and then a sudden change. Her marks fell, she became uncommunicative, stayed out late and announced she was dropping out of school. They did all they could to persuade her to complete her Grade Twelve, but seven weeks ago, only a few days before her seventeenth birthday, she just didn't come home.

"Did you know that she was pregnant?" Maggie asked.

"No. Not right then."

"But she did contact you?" Nat asked.

"Yes. A week ago Saturday." Mrs. Holland brushed her dark hair away from her face. "You can imagine how worried we'd been. We'd called her friends, her school, and finally we called the police."

"You didn't find out she was pregnant until she phoned you?"

Joan glanced at her husband before answering. "Well. Penny Thornton had already told us. Penny's her best friend."

"But only after a lot of persuasion," Eric Holland intervened.

"Tell me about it," Nat said, giving Maggie a nod for her to take notes.

"Well," Joan Holland took a deep breath, "after Amy disappeared, we'd asked Penny several times if she knew what had happened to her. But she always insisted she didn't know anything. In the end, we went to her parents."

"And?" Maggie asked.

"That's when Penny finally broke down and told us Amy was five months' pregnant but had been too scared to tell us."

Joan Holland's voice began to break, and Eric Holland took up the story.

"Apparently, someone had offered to help her go to the States. To some private adoption agency or something like that."

"Five months! Didn't you realize?" Maggie asked.

"She's a very tall, well-built girl," Joan Holland answered, "and you know the styles they wear for school nowadays, large sweaters..." Her voice trailed off.

"And after the adoption?" Nat leaned forward in his seat. "What is supposed to happen afterwards?"

"She's to come home, I suppose." The tears started to pour down Joan Holland's face.

"And you said that you went to the police again when she contacted you?"

"Yes, like I told you. But when we couldn't give them any further details, they said they couldn't help us."

"One more question. This someone who offered to help. Did Penny know who this person was?"

"She said she didn't," Joan grabbed a Kleenex out of a box and balled it in her hand.

"Do you believe her?" Nat asked.

"I'm sure she knows. She and Amy were very close."

Nat stood up. "We need to talk to this Penny."

Joan reached over and picked up a slip of paper from the coffee table. "I thought you would. I've written down her address and phone number." She handed the piece of paper to Nat. "I just pray you can get more out of her than we did."

"May I use your phone?" Nat asked. Eric Holland stood up and led Nat out to the hall.

When the door had closed behind the two men, Maggie asked Joan Holland, "Why wouldn't Amelia tell you she was pregnant?"

Joan looked at the corner of the room. "She was afraid of her father," she whispered.

"Afraid?"

"He was very strict with her. You see, he's a lay preacher at our church, and her getting pregnant goes against all he stands for."

"But he seems resigned to it now."

"Yes." The tears slid unchecked down her cheeks. "You see, she's our only child."

THE DOOR OF THE Thornton house was opened to them by a girl wearing an oversized white sweater. Pushing back a strand of the long, blonde hair that had escaped from her ponytail, she blocked the partly opened doorway. "I've told the Hollands everything I know," she said. "There's no point in going over it again." She started to close the door.

"Penny!" A woman in her mid-forties, wearing grey, paint-splattered slacks and a man's shirt, appeared at the door. "Penny seems to have lost her manners," she said, opening the door wider. "It's Mr. Southby, isn't it? Please come in. I'm Roberta Thornton."

"I *don't* know anything else, Mother!" Penny stormed and headed upstairs.

"Get back here, Penny," her mother ordered, leading Nat and Maggie into the family room, where her husband was seated. Sulkily, Penny followed them.

"Mr. Southby, this is my husband. You spoke to him on the phone."

"Doug Thornton." A dark-haired man got up from his chair and extended his hand to Nat. "Sad affair," he added. "And this is?" he turned toward Maggie.

"My assistant, Maggie Spencer."

Maggie's first impression was of a spaniel, its sad brown eyes peering at her through thick horn-rimmed glasses. He even shook her hand mournfully, and bending down, gathered up his newspaper from his well-worn leather easy chair. "Sit here, Mrs. Spencer," he said. "We'll sit over here on the couch."

"Well, what do you want to know?" Penny said, scowling.

"We'll take it step by step," Nat answered, sitting beside a window overlooking a backyard that had been given over to bicycles, an old sandbox filled with toy trucks and other discarded toys. "Why don't you sit down too, Penny?"

"You the police?" she said nervously, glancing at her parents.

"No. Just trying to find out what's happened to your friend Amy."

"Why?"

"I'm a private investigator," Nat answered shortly.

"Who hired you?"

"When did Amy tell you she was pregnant?" Nat said, ignoring the question.

"I dunno. A long time ago." The girl flung herself into the large leather armchair across from Maggie.

"Did she tell you who the father was?"

"Well . . ." The girl looked at Maggie, who sat taking notes. "Does she have to take down everything I say?"

"Yes," Nat answered. "Strictly for our records. Now . . ."

Penny shifted uncomfortably in her seat, the lock of hair falling across her face again. Absent-mindedly, her fingers began twisting it over and over into a curl. "It was that guy she was seeing."

"Does he have a name?"

She stared out of the window.

"Penny. Answer Mr. Southby," Douglas Thornton intervened.

Maggie got up from her chair and stood beside the girl. "Penny, Amy may be in great danger. We've got to find her."

"Forget it, Maggie," Nat said and stood up dismissively. "She doesn't want to help her friend."

Maggie shot him a look. "Did Amy call you from Seattle, too?" she asked.

"What makes you think that?"

"But she did, didn't she?" Maggie persisted.

"Yeah. But she didn't tell me anything. Get out!" she suddenly shouted. A small boy, his face sticky with jam, was slowly edging into the room.

"Toby, be a good boy and go and see what Josh is doing upstairs," Roberta Thornton said quietly, "after you've washed your hands."

"He won't play with me," the boy said.

"Just get out," Penny yelled. Toby shot his sister a look of hatred and departed.

Nat waited until the child had shut the door. "She must've said something," he continued.

"She was crying," Penny shrugged. "All she said was it wasn't how she thought it was going to be."

"She didn't say anything else?"

"She didn't have time."

"Why not?" Nat asked.

"Someone was coming, so she put the phone down."

"Does she have many boyfriends?" Nat asked.

"She doesn't sleep around, if that's what you mean. She isn't like that."

Douglas Thornton stood up. "Are these sort of questions necessary, Mr. Southby?" he asked testily.

"If we want to find out where the girl's gone, yes."

"But Amy fell in love, didn't she, Penny?" Maggie said, interrupting the two men, who were glaring at each other.

"Yes, but . . ." She looked away, trying not to cry. "She said Derek loved her."

"Derek who?" Nat said.

"Oh shit! Oh shit!"

"Penny!" her father reprimanded.

Penny fished in the pocket of her jeans for a Kleenex and rubbed fiercely at her eyes. "Derek Stone. She said he wanted to get married."

"But Amy didn't want to?" Maggie asked.

"She said they're too young and . . . she's not like me."

"In what way?" Nat asked.

"She's got brains. She wants to go to university."

"But you've got brains," Roberta Thornton said, getting up and putting her arms around her daughter. "You can go to college, too."

"Oh, Mum." Penny wriggled away from her mother. "I'm not clever like Amy."

"Who contacted her at school?" Nat asked.

"Somebody Derek knew."

"You mean another student?"

"No. Derek quit," she said. "It's someone he met where he works."

"Where's that?"

"It's some kind of place where they fix boats and stuff."

"Where is it?"

She shrugged. "Dunno."

"Do you know where he lives?"

"East Vancouver somewhere."

Nat sighed in exasperation. "He's dropped out of school. You don't know where he lives. You don't know where he works. Great!"

"Hey! That's my daughter you're talking to!" Douglas Thornton cut in.

"I'm sorry . . ."

"Can you remember the name of this boatyard?" Maggie asked quickly.

"No, but it's in Richmond somewhere. There's this hamburger joint next door. I know because Amy wanted to get a job there, but her dad wouldn't let her."

"Can you remember the name of the restaurant?" Maggie asked patiently.

"'Captain' something or other."

Nat handed Penny one of his cards. "Call me if you remember anything else. Please."

As they drove away, Maggie turned to Nat with a grin. "So, who did hire you? If I remember rightly, Collins took you off the case."

"It's those girls, Maggie. I've got a gut feeling about them, and the Collins case is smack in the middle of it."

"And what about Bradshaw? His daughter's expecting a report from us."

"You're nagging, Maggie," he said, grinning in spite of himself. "I'll get to that—tomorrow."

AFTER MAGGIE LEFT HIM on Sunday afternoon, Nat had driven to Richmond, and with the help of a telephone directory, found a restaurant called The Captain's Table in Steveston, tucked in beside a small boatyard, both of them overlooking the muddy Fraser River. The diner was an old greasy spoon with the smell of fried onions and french fries permeating the air. Next door was Floyd's Boatyard.

As he walked into the yard, Nat saw a man wearing oily trousers rolled up over black rubber boots, and a large, once white, thick-knit sweater that came down to his knees. On his head was a grease-encrusted fedora. He was delving into the innards of an ancient outboard motor.

"Mr. Floyd?" Nat called out.

"No," the fellow answered without turning around.

"Will he be back soon?"

"Doubt it." He took off his hat and turned around. To Nat's astonishment, the *he* was a *she*, and the woman could have easily doubled for Marie Dressler in *Tugboat Annie*. She looked Nat up and down. "Been dead these past twenty years or more."

"*Mrs.* Floyd?" he asked tentatively.

"Yeah." She picked up an oily rag and turned back to the engine. "Rosie Floyd, that's me. What's it to ya?"

"Does Derek Stone work here?"

"Yeah."

"Is he about?"

"No."

"When will he be in?"

"Who's askin'?"

Nat tried to hand her one of his cards, then changed his mind and read it out to her instead.

"What's he bin up to?"

"I just want to ask him a few questions."

"Be in tomorrow."

"I thought he worked here weekends."

"Hired him full-time." She picked up a screwdriver and attacked the engine once more. "Not much good. But he's learnin'."

"What time tomorrow?"

"You can see him on his break."

"When's that?"

"Ten-thirty." She returned to her work.

MARGARET MADE IT HOME before Harry and his mother, and, putting on an apron, even managed to look domesticated.

"And what's this I hear?" Honoria Spencer greeted her daughter-in-law. "Harry tells me you have a little job."

Margaret shot a withering look at her husband. "Yes, Mother Spencer." She still found it hard to call this woman mother. "I've been working for a couple of months now."

"And what kind of job is it? Harry wasn't very forthcoming."

Who are you kidding? I'll bet he told you every single detail twice to get you primed for the attack! she thought, but she smiled innocently as she said, "Girl Friday."

"Office work?" Harry's mother mulled this over and then she smiled. "You're volunteering. Of course!"

You know damn well I'm not volunteering, you old bitch, Margaret thought. "No, I'm working. In a real office. For real money," she said very pleasantly, then added wickedly, "I work for an investigator."

"My dear, you can't be serious. None of the wives in our family have ever worked for money. And an investigator? You don't mean a detective, do you?" She turned to her son. "She is just joking, Harry, isn't she?"

"No, Mother, she isn't joking."

"The firm is doing well?"

"Quite well, Mother."

"Then I don't understand."

"It's quite simple," Margaret said. "I work because I want to. Now you must excuse me, the dinner is nearly ready." She escaped into the kitchen.

The rest of the evening went fairly well, considering the slight iciness between husband and wife. The subject of the little job was assiduously ignored, and Harry regaled his mother with anecdotes from the office. This the old lady could appreciate. Before he died, Harry's father had been the senior partner in the same firm.

"Your father would be so proud of you, son," she said, wiping her eyes after Harry had told her a long-winded story of old Mr. Hardwick, who was an important client of the firm. "He was one of your father's very first clients."

When Harry finally took his mother home, Margaret washed the dishes, stacked them on the drain tray and went to bed. She did her best to appear fast asleep when he came into the bedroom, but Harry, determined to get in one more lick, announced loudly, "Mother was very upset about your job. She talked of nothing else on the way home."

Tough! thought Margaret, and very soon she really was fast asleep.

As she drove to work the next day, humming along with Frank Sinatra on the radio, she couldn't help grinning as she recalled the look on Honoria Spencer's face when Emily had made her entrance the night before.

"Where did that ... that animal come from?" she had demanded, glaring at Margaret. "You know how allergic Harry and I are to cats."

Emily rubbed herself against Honoria's legs, making the old woman jump out of her seat, before the cat passed her up for the comfort of Harry's lap.

"I think Harry's outgrown his allergy," Margaret said, trying not to laugh.

Harry, looking shame-faced at his mother, handed Emily over to Margaret. "You'd better take her outside, Margaret."

"Get rid of the creature," Honoria had said, settling back into her chair, "or I won't come again."

Margaret knew at that moment that Emily would have a home with her forever.

MAGGIE HAD JUST FINISHED typing up her notes on the interview with Penny Thornton when the telephone rang, and as if on cue, she heard Penny's voice.

"Is that detective there?"

"Not at the moment," Maggie answered. "Will I do?"

There was a long silence, then, "She told me something else on the phone."

"Amy?"

"Yeah. She said they'd never let her come home."

"Who wouldn't?"

"You know, the people at that adoption place."

"Why not?" Maggie kept her voice even. She didn't want the girl to break off the connection. "Why not, Penny?" she repeated.

"Because she saw something."

Maggie felt her patience going. "For heaven's sake, Penny, what did she see?"

"She said she saw them kill this old guy."

Maggie suddenly felt cold. After a pause, she said, "What were her exact words?"

"She said she was waiting for them to come for her in some kinda shed. She said this old guy tried to come in and someone hit him over the head."

"Where was this? Did she say?"

"No. She said when she started to scream, the woman came in and jabbed a needle in her arm."

"Why didn't you tell the police about this?"

"And have them get me, too?"

"Are you calling from school?"

"Yeah. I'm on my break."

"Which school?"

"Kits."

"I'll come and get you."

"No."

"Penny. Do as I say. Wait."

There was a pause, then, "I'm not going to talk to the police."

Maggie left a note for Nat: *Going to Kitsilano High to see Penny. See if you can get Farthing to meet there. Explain later.*

IT WAS A LITTLE AFTER ten thirty that morning before Nat managed to corner Derek Stone. Coke in hand, he was sitting on the end of the dock beyond the boatyard, morosely watching a crowd of gulls fighting over some fish guts on the mudflats below. Nat sat down next to him.

"I'm looking into Amelia Holland's disappearance," he said, after introducing himself.

"I don't know where she is," Derek said, getting up to leave.

"But you did give her a name to contact."

"Yes, but . . . I didn't know the guy." Derek stopped but didn't turn around.

"Who passed the name on to you?" Nat insisted.

"Just some guy who brought his boat in here for repairs."

"Tell me about him."

"He was just a guy." Derek sat again but kept some distance between himself and Nat. "See, Amy'd been bugging me. Heck, how'd I know if I really was the father?"

"Okay. This guy," Nat prompted.

"Well, it was over a few beers, see. I told him about her bugging me."

"And?"

"He said he knew someone."

"What was the guy's name?" Nat persisted.

"He was just a guy."

"You can do better than that, Derek."

"Larry something," he mumbled.

"For God's sake, man! What was his other name?"

"I told you we just got talking over a couple of beers."

"How was Amy to make contact?"

"He gave me a phone number."

"You still got it?"

"I gave it to Amy."

"Did she meet the guy?"

"She's gone, isn't she?"

"Derek, think! Did she say where she was meeting him?"

"Derek," boomed Rosie's voice, "you can yap to that guy on yer own time."

Derek stood up. "I've got to go."

Nat stood up, too. "I think you're holding back on me." He started for his car.

Derek walked toward the yard and then turned back. "They were going to help her, right?"

Nat stopped in his tracks. "So?"

"So why did Larry want to know so much?"

"Know so much?"

"Heck, you know—did she sleep around? What kind of house did she live in? Were her folks professionals . . . that kinda stuff."

"Derek!" Rosie yelled. "Yer'll be working on your lunch hour if ya don't git a move on."

"I've got to go."

"Call me," Nat said, thrusting the last of his crumpled business cards into Derek's hand.

He was still mulling over his talk with Derek as he entered the office. "Maggie, I'm back," he called. No Maggie! He peered inside his own office. "Where the hell is she?" Then he saw her note on his desk. "My God, woman, what have you done this time?" He lifted the receiver and dialed Farthing's number.

IT TOOK MAGGIE five minutes to get from the office at Broadway and Granville to Kitsilano High, but another ten minutes trying to find somewhere to park. She ran through the old school's front entrance and then came to a complete stop. Where could she expect to find the girl? The administration office was to her right.

She waited impatiently for the faded blonde sitting behind the desk to take notice of her. "Yes?" the woman said finally.

"Penny Thornton, where can I find her?"

The woman glanced at the oversized clock on the wall. "In class. Why?"

"She called me. I must speak to her."

"Are you her mother?"

"No. I just need to speak to her."

"I think you'd better see the principal, Mrs. . . . ."

"Spencer. Yes, right away, and please get Penny in here, too."

"I can't do that without permission from Mr. Harding." She rose, moved at a leisurely pace across the room and opened a glass-panelled door. "There's a Mrs. Spencer to see you, Mr. Harding . . . She says it's important . . . It's to do with Penny Thornton." She turned to Maggie. "He can give you five minutes."

But it took longer than five minutes to convince a very stern Mr. Harding that it was imperative that Penny be allowed to come out of class. After he had examined Maggie's driver's licence, he called Nat's office—even though she explained that he wouldn't be there.

"I think I'd better contact the girl's parents," Mr. Harding said, reaching for the phone.

"Please, Mr. Harding," Maggie pleaded, "hear me out. Penny has information on Amelia Holland's disappearance."

"All the more reason to call her parents."

"When Penny phoned, she asked me specifically not to tell her parents," Maggie said, fishing in her handbag for a slip of paper. "Here, this is Sergeant Farthing's phone number at the Vancouver Police Station. May I call him?"

Harding took the piece of paper from her and reached for the telephone. "I'll call him," he declared. Maggie listened while Harding had a short conversation with Farthing. "Yes, sergeant," he said in a resigned voice. "I understand. We'll send for the girl when you arrive." He put the phone down and turned to Maggie. "He's coming here to the school. I will put our guidance counsellor's room at his disposal."

"Thank you." She picked up her bag and turned to go out.

"You can wait in the staff room. Mrs. Jansen will show you the way and call you when they arrive." Maggie felt herself dismissed.

As the door closed behind her, Harding reached for the phone.

In the staff room, Maggie helped herself to a cup of tepid coffee and dutifully put a dime into the cracked saucer sitting beside the pot. While she waited, she watched the schoolyard from the window, but it was at least thirty minutes before Farthing arrived, accompanied by a policewoman. Moments later a taxi drew up and Nat jumped out.

"But I told you I didn't want to see the police," Penny complained as she and Maggie were escorted to the counsellor's office.

"All you have to do is tell them what you told me over the telephone," Maggie said, pushing the girl into the room.

It took a few false starts and a bit of prodding from Maggie before Penny would tell Farthing and Nat about the conversation she'd had with Amelia Holland. She sat as close to Maggie as she could, but Maggie had to admit that Farthing did a good job of interviewing the girl. The policewoman sat behind Penny, taking notes. They had just about finished when the door burst open and a distraught Roberta Thornton rushed into the room.

"Penny!" she cried, going to her daughter. "What's happened?" She turned to Farthing. "What's going on?"

"It's okay, Mrs. Thornton," Maggie said. "Penny very sensibly got in touch with me when she remembered something Amy had told her."

"But, Penny, why didn't you tell *me*?"

"You'd only've got into a state, Mum!"

"Is this something you didn't tell the Hollands?" Roberta asked, sitting down next to her daughter. Penny shook her head. "But Penny, you swore you didn't know . . ." Roberta said sadly.

"Don't worry, Mrs. Thornton," Maggie interrupted.

"Perhaps we can get on," Farthing said, tapping his pen on the table. Then, turning toward the girl, "Now, everything from the beginning again, please."

"Not again!" The girl wailed, but after a look from her mother, she started over.

"What I can't understand," Farthing said when she finished, "is why didn't you come forward right after she phoned."

"They might come after me."

"Who'll come after her?" Roberta cried, jumping up from her seat.

"Please, Mrs. Thornton," Farthing said, "let's get all the information before we get excited, shall we? Now Penny, this is very important, have you told anyone else about Amelia seeing the old man killed?"

Penny shook her head. "No, like I told you, I was too scared. But I keep thinking about it."

"What made you tell Mrs. Spencer?"

"Yes, I'd like to know that, too," Roberta cut in.

Penny looked at Maggie. "She came to the house, see, with him." She pointed at Nat. "I thought she'd understand," she said, gazing miserably out of the window.

"She did the right thing, you know, calling us," Maggie said.

"But those people . . ." Penny cried.

"If you're sure you haven't told anyone else, they can't hurt you." Farthing stood up. "Now I want you to go back to your class and try and forget it."

As Penny walked toward the door, she turned to Maggie. "Everybody's going to wonder why I was called down here."

Maggie smiled at her. "I'm sure you'll think of something."

Roberta Thornton stood up. "I'd better go with her." She turned and glared at Farthing. "You'd better be right. If anything should happen..."

"That's all we need, a hysterical mother," Farthing said as he struggled into his suede jacket. "I want to see you two back at the station." He snapped his briefcase shut and stalked out of the room.

"You came in a taxi, Nat?" Maggie probed as they left the schoolyard.

"Yeah. I dropped the car off for an oil change on the way back to the office. Then I found your note."

"Mine's around the corner." As she put the car into gear, she said, "You know that the old man was Ernie, don't you?"

"What makes you so sure?"

"Ernie was killed about the same time that Amelia went missing. March 23rd."

"But we don't know whether the old man she saw getting killed was here or in Seattle."

"No, but I think Collins and Violet are mixed up in it somehow." She drove without speaking for a few minutes, then, "Where were you this morning?"

"Looking for Derek Stone."

"Amelia's so-called boyfriend?"

"I found him, too." He related his conversation with Derek. "It's too much of a coincidence that there could be two Larrys mixed up in this. First there was Larry Longhurst taking Collins' boat, and he had a pregnant girl with him. Then we find another Larry mixed up with Amelia. Also pregnant."

"And that brings us back to Collins and Violet," Maggie said as they drew up outside the precinct.

"Why?" Nat asked.

"Because Collins has something going with Violet."

"Well, of course, she's his aunt..."

"And where did Emily go every time she went wandering?" Maggie asked triumphantly.

"What's the cat got to do with it?"

"That's where Ernie went. To look for his cat."

"So?"

"So he got killed at Violet's," Maggie concluded as she switched off the engine.

"Maybe."

"Look. He must have gone after Emily, heard something or saw something and... and they killed him." She picked up her handbag and opened her door. "Come on. Let's face the music."

"Don't say anything to Farthing about this, eh Maggie?" Nat said as he stepped out of the car. "Let's talk it over some more first."

In Nat's former office, Sergeant Farthing spent twenty minutes ranting and raving about their interference in police business and failure to keep him informed.

"But Maggie did bring you in on the Thornton girl's statement," Nat argued. "What more do you want?"

"Just as well she did," Farthing said, glaring at them both. "So what else have you got to tell me?"

Nat thought for a minute. If he told Farthing about Derek, perhaps he would get some feedback on Larry Longhurst. Was it worth the risk? He decided it was. "I've been following up on Amelia's boyfriend, Derek Stone."

"Who?"

"You haven't interviewed him on Amelia's disappearance?"

"No reason to. Up to this afternoon, I knew nothing about the girl. She comes under Missing Persons."

"Well," Nat said slowly, "you may be interested to know that Derek mentioned a Larry. And it seems very likely it's our friend Longhurst."

Farthing looked thoughtful. "Okay, give me all you've got," he answered reluctantly.

"What's happened to Longhurst?" Nat countered. "Last I heard he was badly injured."

"He was. He's out of hospital and we've questioned him."

"How'd he explain about the accident?" Nat asked.

"The matter's still under investigation," Farthing said shortly, and shifted uncomfortably in his chair. "And frankly, it's none of your business."

"I guess you don't want to know about Derek Stone, then?" Nat stood up. "Come on, Maggie, we've got work to do."

"Sit down, sit down."

Nat sat and leaned forward. "So how did he explain the accident?"

"At first he insisted he knew nothing about June Cosgrove. Then we produced the life jacket the girl was wearing."

"Did he say how the boat was wrecked?" Maggie asked.

"He said he'd borrowed the boat to take the girl over to a party on one of the islands. Then the weather turned nasty. She panicked and the boat capsized."

"Did you believe him?"

"No. Now tell me about this Derek character. Where will I find him?"

"Quit screwing around, Farthing," Nat said. "We're talking about a girl's life."

Farthing swung his swivel chair around to face the window and thoughtfully tapped a pencil against his teeth. "Your information better be good," he said eventually. "There were bullet holes in the hull."

"Bullet holes?"

"We figured they might've come from the US Coast Guard. They admit they shot at a boat that refused to stop."

"How did Larry explain that?"

"He changed his story a bit then and said he must've gone too close to the border, and that's when the girl started to panic. The boat started sinking and when he tried to beach it, he hit a reef."

"Was there anything in the boat when you found it?"

"Look, Southby, I've told you enough. I don't like dealing with people like you, so get out."

"What the hell do you mean by *people like me?*" Nat exploded, and jumping to his feet, he leaned over Farthing's desk. "What are you getting at, Farthing?"

"I don't like ex-cops, especially ones on the ta . . ."

"What the hell are you implying . . . ?" Nat broke off as he felt Maggie's hand tugging at his arm.

"Leave it, Nat," she said quietly and gently pulled him toward the door.

After they had left, Farthing slowly opened the bottom drawer of his desk and removed a half sheet of paper from a buff folder. "A bit more evidence and I've got you, Southby," he muttered, scanning the paper once again. "You conniving son of a bitch." He carefully placed the note back in the folder and returned it to the drawer.

"What's with that guy?" Nat fumed when they reached Maggie's car. "Every time I see him, he makes some kind of crack." He opened the passenger door and flung himself into the seat. "There's something strange going on."

"He certainly seems to have it in for you," Maggie answered thoughtfully. "Why don't you give your pal Sawasky a call?" she added. "Perhaps he could shed some light."

"I think I might just do that," Nat answered her.

Fifteen minutes later, Maggie parked the Morris in front of the Aristocrat Restaurant just down the street from the office. "Lunch is on me," she announced. She waited until their order arrived before she returned to the topic of Collins' and Violet's involvement in Ernie's death. "It's the only logical explanation," she said briskly.

"But what could Ernie have overheard? I can't see old Violet as a gangster type, and she'd hardly have killed him just so she could keep Emily."

She took a sip of her coffee before answering. "I've been mulling it over and over in my mind." She put the cup carefully back in its saucer. "It's got to do with these pregnant girls, Nat."

"Pregnant girls?" Nat waved his cup in the direction of the elusive waitress. "As far as I can see, only two of those missing girls were pregnant—June Cosgrove and Amy Holland."

"Three," she replied quietly.

"Would you folks like some more coffee?" the waitress said as she slapped the bill down in front of Nat.

"It's about time..." He caught Maggie's disapproving eye. "Yes, please," he said, pushing his cup toward the girl. "What do you mean, three?" he said, turning back to Maggie just as she picked up the bill. "And give me that, by the way."

"No, I have it. Now listen, I saw another pregnant girl entering Violet's house, remember?"

"When was this?"

"About three weeks ago when I went to see how Emily was doing. It didn't mean much to me at the time. I thought she must be Violet's daughter or maybe granddaughter."

"I suppose there's a remote chance that you're right." Nat leaned forward and laid his hand over hers. "Promise me you won't go there again."

Maggie looked down at the large protective hand covering hers and gently pulled hers away. "I think it's time we were on our way." And she headed for the cash register.

"WHERE HAVE YOU BEEN?" Harry's querulous voice met her as she entered the house. "I've been alone here for at least an hour."

"I didn't know you were coming home early," Margaret said, slipping off her coat. "Something wrong?" Emily, who had been curled up on Harry's lap, stretched, arched her back and jumped down to run into the kitchen.

"I'm coming down with the flu," Harry stated.

"Would you like me to make you some tea?"

"No. Miss Fitch-Smythe could see I wasn't well. She very kindly went out and bought me some Aspirin tablets." He pulled himself wearily out of the armchair. "I'm going to bed."

"Good idea, Harry. I'll bring you a hot water bottle."

"Margaret." He was halfway up the stairs, looking down at her. "You've changed." He coughed and blew his nose into his spotless handkerchief. "You've got to give it up, you know." He climbed a few more stairs. "I've never felt so alone. You should be at home, especially when I'm sick."

Poor old Harry. Margaret carefully filled his favourite hot water bottle and screwed the cap on tightly. *He's right. We can't go on like this much longer.* Hot water bottle in hand, she trudged reluctantly up the stairs. Emily, tail on high, followed closely behind.

CHAPTER TWELVE

The rest of the week flew by, and before Maggie knew it, it was Thursday again. That morning, Nat wrote a letter to Mrs. Read, apologizing for the slow progress he was making in the investigation of her father's death. He didn't bother to tell her that the old man hadn't been particularly liked by his neighbours, who seemed to have forgotten him already. He finished up the report by asking if she, Mrs. Read, still wanted him to continue with the investigation.

"I still think," Maggie said, placing the typed sheet in front of him, "that we've got to start looking closer at Collins and Violet."

"Oh, come off it," he replied, scrawling his signature at the bottom of the page. "Quit casting poor old Violet as a heavy."

At noon she gathered all the outgoing mail, picked up her handbag and poked her head into Nat's office. "I'm on my way."

He looked up from the document he was reading. "Can you be here about eight-thirty tomorrow?" he asked.

"I suppose so." She waited.

"Thought we'd get through the office work early and take a run over to the Osprey Harbour Yacht Club."

Maggie raised her eyebrows. "Hoping to see Collins?"

He grinned at her. "You never know. Anyway, I'll give Cubby

a call and maybe we can have lunch with him in the clubhouse. Okay?"

"Okay by me," she said, smiling back at him.

He picked up his pen and resumed writing. *She's a hell of an attractive woman when she smiles.*

IT WAS ANOTHER PERFECT west-coast day. Sitting in Nat's car, Maggie felt herself relaxing. Her husband had got over his flu bout quite quickly the previous week and returned to the office and his attentive secretary. But the atmosphere at home had remained heavy, their relations awkward.

The repaired, newly painted *Seagull*, bobbing up and down in the gentle swell, was back at her berth. Phillip Collins, screwdriver in hand, was on his knees, fixing something under one of the seats in the front cockpit. "Hi. Got a minute?" Nat called out.

"Oh, it's you," Collins said, getting to his feet.

"Boat looks lovely," Maggie said. "Take you long to fix it?"

"Long enough," he answered shortly. "I could kill the little bugger."

"How is Larry?"

"Mending and very subdued."

"Did he ever tell you why he took *Seagull* out that night?" Nat asked.

"No."

"He must have given some explanation," Nat insisted.

"Even if he did, it's none of your business, Southby. Case closed."

"Did you know Ernie Bradshaw?" Nat asked.

"No, who's he?"

"The old guy who was murdered a few weeks back. He knew your Aunt Violet."

"Oh, that Ernie. The guy with the cat. I never met him."

"Mr. Collins," Maggie cut in. "Your aunt's got a garage in her backyard."

"A garage?" He stared at Maggie, mystified. "Yes. So what?"

"Ernie Bradshaw's cat used to hole up somewhere. I just wondered if that's where . . ." Her voice tapered off.

"If you're so interested, Mrs. Spencer, why don't you go ask Violet?" Turning his back on them, he knelt again and became absorbed in his work.

There was no sign of the owners of *Flying Fancy*. She was still berthed next to *Seagull*, silently waiting and tightly covered against the elements. "Have to come down one weekend," Nat said as they walked back along the float. "I'd like to have another little chat with Sylvia and her mate."

"Who are they?"

"*Seagull*'s neighbours," he explained. "You'd love 'em." He took Maggie's arm. "Come on, let's have a quick tour around the yard before we meet Cubby."

Later, sipping a large gin and tonic, Maggie looked out of the clubhouse window. "They're so beautiful," she said wistfully.

Nat looked at her. *And so are you*, he thought, but he said, "What? The boats?" He wrenched his mind back to follow her gaze. "Got to solve a lot more cases before the agency can have one of those." He grinned. "Here's Cubby at last." He stood up and waved his friend over to the table.

Immaculate in whites and more tanned than ever, Cubby breezed over to where they were sitting. "Ordered yet?"

"No, waited for you."

After they had been served, Nat turned to Cubby. "I see Collins has fixed his boat."

"Yep, I guess his insurance coughed up." Cubby took a mouthful of curried shrimp. "Must have cost a packet, though, the way it was banged up."

"Did they ever find out what happened?" Maggie picked up her seafood club sandwich and took a bite.

"I think it was just a joy ride." Cubby turned to Nat. "How's business treating the great tec?"

"We're getting there," Nat answered. "Still can't take Fridays off to play boats like some people I know."

"Let me tell you, it's taken a lot of hard work." It occurred to Nat that he had no idea what Cubby did for a living, and it was on the tip of his tongue to ask, but Cubby had already turned to Maggie. "Dessert?"

"Just coffee," she answered.

Sipping her coffee, she listened to the two men talking over their school days. Nat, smoking a small brown cheroot, glanced up and saw her looking at him.

"Gave the cigars up just for you," he explained with a grin, waving the cheroot in the air.

"You ever smoked cigars?" Maggie asked Cubby.

"No. Like everyone, I tried cigarettes when I was young." He reached over for a third tub of cream. "My only real vice is gallons of cream in my coffee. Can't understand how anyone can drink it black. How about you, Maggie? Any bad habits?"

"I've never smoked, but I love chocolate. And I'd love a boat like yours."

"All the good things in life," he said, as he stirred his coffee. "What about adventure?"

"Until I started working for Nat, my life had been pretty dull."

"Aha," Cubby said, raising his eyebrows at Nat.

"Down, boy," Nat said, laughing. "Maggie's my right arm, and she's turning out to be a helluva good investigator."

Maggie's high spirits stayed with her until she reached home and parked, but the prospect of the weekend with a resentful Harry sobered her up fast. *What am I going to do?* She carried her bags of groceries through the back door into the kitchen and bent down to stroke Emily, who had come to meet her. "Well, at least he's accepted *you*, puss."

While she packed the groceries away, her mind went back to the pleasant lunch with the two men. But something bothered her, and for the life of her she couldn't think what it was. *Was it something Nat said? No. Or maybe something Cubby said?* She went over the conversation and the bantering between the two men. Emily, fed up with waiting for supper, stretched up and clawed Maggie's leg. "Okay, you're next," she said as she bent down to fill the cat's bowl with kibble. Emily just blinked her blue eyes at Maggie and proceeded to her dish.

The beautiful weather continued, and on Saturday morning the garden called for attention. She loved the feel of the earth as she transplanted seedlings, pulled weeds and pruned the roses. Even Harry was happy. He liked to see his wife doing things around the house and garden, and he even got the mower out of the garden shed and cut the grass. While she worked, she went over the lunch with Nat and Cubby once again bit by bit, searching for a clue to what was niggling at her. Then suddenly it came to her. She waited until Harry had started on the front lawn before slipping into the house and dialing Nat's number.

"It's Maggie," she said.

"What's up?"

"Wanted to thank you for lunch. I enjoyed it."

"Me too." He waited for her to continue.

"You've known Cubby a long time . . ."

"Since high school."

"You've kept in touch all that time?"

"Not really, no. He hung around with a different gang, and his old man had enough dough to send him to UBC. I joined the force. Why?"

"How well do you know him now?"

He was slow answering her. "To tell the truth, up to now, our paths rarely crossed. Why the sudden interest?"

"Do you remember him telling us how he likes cream in his coffee?"

"Yeah, but . . . ?" Nat asked in a baffled tone.

"Margaret, what have you done with the garden shears?" Harry poked his head into the kitchen. "Oh sorry, I didn't hear the phone."

"Thanks again." She replaced the receiver and turned to Harry. "I had to call Nat to remind him of something for tomorrow. The shears? I'm sure you'll find them in the shed. I'll come and look."

"I should have known it was too good to be true!" Harry stalked outside. "Never mind! I'll find them myself."

"Oh, damn all men!" She ran up the stairs, pulled off her gardening clothes and ran a hot shower.

"Now, what was that all about?" Nat said, replacing the phone. "Why would Maggie call me to ask about Cubby?" He picked up his newspaper. "She can't be interested in him . . ." Rattled, he put on his jacket and headed out for a walk.

MARGARET AND HARRY were extremely polite to each other for the rest of the day. She felt as if she was walking on eggshells and studiously avoided any mention of her job. At breakfast on Sunday morning, Harry put down his newspaper, removed his reading glasses and said, "Margaret, I've been thinking about our problem."

"Which problem is that, Harry?"

"I understand you feel loyalty to this man, so I think it only fair that you give him a month's notice."

"A month's notice?"

"Yes. That way he can find a person of his own sort to help him."

"What do you mean, his own sort?"

"You know perfectly well what I mean. His own class of person, if you like."

"That's nice of you, Harry. But I don't think so."

"You mean he won't want a month's notice?"

"No. For the last time, you'll just have to accept the fact that I like this job and I need it. And I don't intend to give it up." To her humiliation, she felt tears running down her face, and she turned and ran from the room.

By the evening, Margaret found the tension between them unbearable. So while Harry watched the *Ed Sullivan Show*, she put on a beige sweater and slacks, a matching jacket and white running shoes and then knotted her favourite silk scarf around her neck. Before slipping out of the house, she dialed Nat's number, but when there was no answer, she left a message with the answering service. Climbing into her car, she drove aimlessly for awhile, feeling the peace of solitude, and when she had calmed down again, she realized that she was driving past Violet Larkfield's house. It was in total darkness.

She stopped the car a few houses down the street, parked, and then, taking a small flashlight out of the glove compartment and pushing it into her coat pocket, walked back toward the house. A half moon showing through the scudding clouds made the swaying trees and bushes cast ghostly shadows in the gardens. Maggie shivered. She started to lift the latch of the gate, then stopped, remembering how it squeaked. Although there seemed to be no sign of life, she decided to play it safe. The house stood on a large corner lot facing Seventh Avenue, with the entrance to the garage coming off Larch Street. Her flashlight showing the way, Maggie rounded the corner and turned into the driveway, stepping lightly on the gravel leading to the garage that loomed in the dark. She followed the path beside it, and using her flashlight, peered into the small side window. The garage was empty. Violet must be out.

Using less caution, she walked through the mud to the rear of the building. There, built onto its back wall, was a lean-to extension. *A potting shed?* She played the beam of her torch on its small window, but although she pressed her face close to the glass, the weak light could give her no indication of the interior. She tried the handle of the door. It wouldn't budge, but her flashlight showed that the key had been left in the lock. Just as she reached out for it, a car swung into the driveway and its high beams flooded the garden with light. Heart hammering, she turned the key and slipped inside the shed. Keeping the door open a crack, she watched two shadowy figures pass by and approach the rear of the house. *Thank God, they're going inside.*

"The girl's not here yet?" a man's voice enquired.

I know that voice, Maggie thought.

"About an hour's time."

And that's Violet.

"The place is ready, so you can give me a hand with the bedding," Violet continued.

"Right, but hurry up. I haven't got all night."

"You're one inconsiderate bastard," Violet snarled. "Go open the door. I left the key in the lock."

Maggie froze. She didn't dare risk the flashlight to find a hiding place, so she pressed herself against the wall behind the door and hoped she would be able to slip out.

The strong beam of light raked the front of the shed. "The door's open."

"It can't be."

"You must've left it open."

"I did not," Violet asserted.

Maggie's legs felt like jelly as the door was flung back onto her and the light from the overhead fixture fell full onto her stricken face.

"Well, well! How nice to see you again, Mrs. Spencer," John Cuthbertson said, before turning to Violet. "Maggie and I had a most enjoyable lunch together on Friday."

"Emily escaped this afternoon. I just thought there might be a possibility..."

"Come, come, Maggie my dear," Cuthbertson interrupted her. "You can do better than that." He took a step toward her. Maggie tried to push her way past him, but he grabbed her arm, twisting it behind her back, and forced her face down onto the bed.

"Nat knows I'm here!" she yelled at the man as she struggled to break his hold.

"On a Sunday night? I don't think so," he answered in an infuriating sarcastic drawl.

"And so does my husband," she finished up lamely.

"I warned you she was getting too nosy," Violet said from the doorway. "Now what are we going to do?"

"Oh, I'll think of something!"

"Well, you'd better start thinking quick!"

"No problem, Mrs. L." He transferred his weight, putting his knee into Maggie's back while he fished in his pocket. "Take my car keys and open the trunk."

"I'll get some rope," Violet said.

This can't be happening! Maggie squirmed beneath Cuthbertson's weight. But all this did was to make him push her face harder into the mattress.

"Violet dear, do as I say and open the trunk."

Fury gave Maggie new strength, and twisting her body, she broke free, pushing Cuthbertson back and making for the open door. The last thing she saw was Violet's fist coming straight toward her face.

Violet stood over Maggie's prostrate body. "So what are you going to do with her now?"

"No problem, my dear," said Cuthbertson. "Our nosy little friend here is going for a swim. A *long* swim."

HER HEAD POUNDING, Maggie forced her eyes open and quickly shut them again. Something was very wrong. She willed herself to fight the nausea and open her eyes again. *My God, I'm blind.* She put out her arms and touched metal. It was then that she felt the movement of travelling and the smell of gas. *Oh God! I'm in the trunk of a car! It must be Cuthbertson's Mercedes!* As she felt claustrophobic panic rising, she started to retch, then mercifully blacked out once more.

The next time Maggie woke, it was to a gentle rocking motion, and over it she heard the throb of an engine. Her head and right arm ached and she felt very nauseous, but it was too much effort to open her eyes. Then the horror of being in the trunk of the car came back to her, and forcing her eyes open, she struggled to sit up, but the straps binding her to the narrow bunk held her down. Daylight filtering through a small round window beside her made her realize where she was. *I'm on a boat. Where are they taking me?* She closed her eyes again and tried to think. Slowly, she pieced the events together: her argument with Harry, leaving home, finding the small room behind Violet's garage and . . . Cold fear engulfed her again as she relived the scene with Violet and John Cuthbertson. She struggled against the straps and tried to call out, but only a rasping sound came from her dry throat. *I have to escape. I've got to warn Nat.* She felt herself drifting.

"The cops?" John Cuthbertson's voice jolted her awake. "I thought they were finished with him!" she heard him say.

"They asked him about the Cosgrove girl again," another voice answered through a splatter of static.

That's Violet's voice, Maggie thought.

"And they wanted to know if he knew Sally Fielding."

They must be talking on the radio.

"Shit!" Cuthbertson snarled.

"You've got to come back and get this girl out of here. She's ready to pop anytime."

"Send Larry with her in your car."

"Can't risk it," Violet's voice crackled. "He says the cops are following him ... You're going ... have to ... take ..." Her voice faded.

"Damn! Speak up," he shouted irritably. "Will the little punk spill?"

"No, not Larry, he's ..." Maggie strained to hear the answer.

"All right, all right," Cuthbertson yelled back irritably over the static. "But we may need bargaining power. I'll delay dumping the goods overboard and take it to the cabin instead, then come back for the girl."

"Do you ... that's wise?" the voice faded away.

"I make the decisions around here!" Cuthbertson slammed the receiver down. "Bloody hell! They've screwed it up again!"

Maggie struggled to stay awake and make sense of the conversation, but it was no use, and she drifted off again. When she awoke again, the boat engine was silent, and she opened her eyes to see Cuthbertson bending over her. "Where am I?"

"What a classic question! You disappoint me, Maggie." He bent to untie the straps and pull her into a sitting position. "Get up."

"Please. I need some water," Maggie's voice rasped.

"Get up!"

She tried to stand, but the cabin whirled around her and she fell back onto the bunk. He put his arm around her waist. "Come on, up onto the deck."

The house on the cliff high above the dock was a two-storyed structure set among tall pines and cedars. Maggie stalled, even sitting down on the path leading up the steep slope, but John Cuthbertson twisted her arm behind her back and literally pushed her along in front of him. Stopping only to unlock the front door, he propelled her up the front stairs, finally thrusting her into a large bedroom on the second floor. Although she had put up a good fight all the way, he still managed to throw her on the single bed and jab another needle into her arm.

HARRY SWITCHED OFF the television and looked at his watch. Eleven o'clock. Where had Margaret got to with his hot chocolate? Pushing himself up from his chair, he went into the kitchen. The house seemed strangely quiet. Even Emily was asleep in her basket. "Margaret?" he called. *I suppose she's not talking to me. Well, two can play at that game.* He reached into the cupboard for the tin of chocolate and put the kettle on. Carrying his cup gingerly up the stairs, he pushed open the door to their room. "I've made my own chocolate. I don't know if you . . ." His voice trailed off. The bedroom was empty. "Sulking in the spare room, I suppose," he muttered. He got ready for bed.

There was no aromatic smell of coffee wafting up the stairs when he woke the next morning. In fact, the house still had the same eerie silence about it. He showered, dressed and went down to the kitchen. Emily stretched, arched her back and walked sedately to the back door, which he obediently opened for her. *Why isn't Margaret up? She'd never be late for that job of hers. She must've overslept.* He walked back to the hall, struggled into his coat and picked up his briefcase. "Don't worry about my breakfast," he called up the stairs, his voice dripping sarcasm. "I'll get it downtown."

Opening the double garage door, he saw that Margaret's car was missing. "I have it," he said triumphantly. "She wants to worry me and she's gone to Barbara's." And carefully placing his case on the passenger seat, he backed his own car out.

THE DOOR TO THE OFFICE was still locked, and Nat looked at his watch as he fished in his pocket for his keys. *Unusual for Maggie to be late.* He threw his hat in the direction of the coat tree, but it wasn't as much fun without Maggie's disapproving look. He closed his office door and was soon immersed in work. The phone rang three times before he realized that Maggie wasn't going to pick it up. It was Cubby on the line. "You're up early," Nat said. "What can I do for you?"

"Just thought I'd tell you how much I enjoyed Friday's lunch."

"Me too," Nat answered. "And I know Maggie did."

"By the way, how's that Longhurst business going?"

"Not well," Nat answered. "Why?"

"Bloody fool taking Collins' boat like that. Deserves all he gets." He paused. "Give my best to Mrs. Spencer."

"Thanks, I will."

Nat replaced the receiver and flung open the door. "Maggie," he called. He stopped short and looked at his watch. "She's never this late." He reached for the phone. *I'll call the answering service and see if she left a message,* he thought. "Yes," the operator replied to his enquiry, "you have three messages. Mr. Matthew Oates reminding you about your golf date; Mr. Pickering, he says you have his number, called for an appointment; and the last one was from your secretary." She paused for breath. "She said she'd tried to call you at your home but you were out, so she had called the office in the hope that you might be there. Anyway," the woman finished up, "Mrs. Spencer said it was something important she had to tell you, but it could wait till the morning."

Nat thanked her and quickly dialed Maggie's home phone. "Answer, Maggie! Answer, dammit!" But the ringing continued.

He slammed the phone down and strode back to his own office. "Accident. She must've been in an accident."

He reached for the phone again and dialed the police. But as far as they knew, she had not been involved in any accident. *There's nothing for it, I'll have to call her husband.* He found Harry's office number neatly entered into the Rolodex. But it seemed to take forever to get past the guardian secretary.

"If my wife's not in your office this morning," Harry answered Nat's query, "it's because she's come to her senses and taken my advice."

"And what advice was that, Mr. Spencer?" Nat asked, his hackles rising.

"To give up that... that inappropriate position with you, of course."

"Did Maggie tell you she was giving up her job?"

There was a long silence on the other end of the line before Harry answered. "My wife knows my wishes."

"Why didn't Maggie tell me herself?"

"Margaret is visiting our daughter. Now, Mr. Southby, I have work to do." The line went dead.

"Pompous bastard," he said, pacing the room. "Something's bloody well wrong. She would've phoned. She wouldn't just walk out on me." Then a thought hit him and he stopped pacing. "Maybe that's what she was calling about!" he started rummaging through the desk drawers. "Dammit! I don't even know her daughter's name." He pulled the bottom drawer right out, and papers, notebooks, pens and pencils spilled onto the floor. "And I know that son of a bitch won't give it to me."

HARRY SPENCER SAT HOLDING the telephone in his hand, his index finger poised over the dial. "No, I won't give her the satisfaction," he muttered and replaced it on the cradle.

EMILY WAS WAITING on the doorstep when Harry arrived home. She mewed impatiently, reaching up to him while he fumbled for his keys. "She hasn't come back, then?" He followed the cat into the cold, empty house. After he'd removed his coat, brushed Emily's hairs off his pants, taken his briefcase into the study and gone through the mail, he walked into the kitchen. Emily stretched up and clawed his leg. "I suppose you're hungry." He pushed her down. She looked up at him expectantly as he opened all the cupboards to find the cat food. With Emily satisfied, he wandered back into the hall and climbed the stairs to see if there was any sign of Margaret. But the house was still.

After washing down a cheese sandwich supper with a cup of instant coffee, Harry decided that Margaret's place was definitely at home with him. He would have to swallow his pride, but he sat looking at the phone for quite awhile before dialing Barbara's number.

"Hello, Barbara. I would like to speak to your mother."

"Mother?" Barbara answered in surprise. "Why would she be here?"

"She's a little late. I thought perhaps she called in to see you."

"Mother is not in the habit of dropping in, Father," Barbara said icily. "Perhaps she's gone to see Grandmother. Why don't you call her?"

"Perhaps I will," he answered and replaced the receiver. But he knew it was very unlikely that his wife would have gone to his mother's. The only other place was Mildred's, in New Westminster. He dialed the number.

"Hello," a man's voice answered.

"I wish to speak to Mildred."

"Mildred? Oh, you mean Midge. She's making supper; hold on a sec." He could hear murmuring in the background.

"Father?" Midge's voice sounded wary.

"Mildred, is your mother there?"

"Mother? You two had a fight?"

"That's neither here nor there," he answered abruptly. "It's just that she's late home and she's not at Barbara's."

"Did she say she would be late?"

"Uh, no," Harry answered stiffly.

"You have had a fight, haven't you?"

"Just a few words," he admitted reluctantly.

"Have you phoned her office?" Midge asked, then, "Jason, watch those spuds. They're boiling over."

"I can see you're busy," Harry said.

"No, don't go, Father. What exactly did she say this morning?"

"I didn't actually see her this morning," he mumbled.

"You mean she wasn't up?"

"Don't worry," he said hastily, before Midge could ask any more awkward questions. "She's sure to call."

Midge walked back into her kitchen, a worried look on her face. "I think Mum has up and left him."

"No, not your mother," Jason answered. "She's one of the few remaining 'stiff upper lips.' She'd stick it out whatever."

"I'm not so sure," Midge answered. "She's changed a lot since she's had that job. No, something's happened. I'm going to call Barbara."

Harry's annoyance increased. This was so unlike Margaret. Perhaps he should call the police? But they would ask awkward questions, such as when had he last seen her. And he would look foolish having to admit that it was sometime after supper on Sunday. And he didn't even know if she had come back, or if she had really slept in the spare room. *The spare room* . . . He raced up the stairs and flung the door open. The bed was neatly made up, guest towels on it and absolutely no sign that Margaret had slept there the previous night. He sat down on the bed and put his head in his hands. *I'll have to call that Southby fellow—but I don't even know his number.*

IT WAS AFTER 6:30, and Nat sat glumly looking at the phone. "Do I ring that stuffed shirt again or not?" Except for Harry's, he'd been unable to find any of Maggie's personal phone numbers when he'd ransacked her desk. "No. What I've got to do is to go around to the house and face that son of a bitch. And he'd better give me some straight answers."

MAGGIE'S HEAD FELT LIKE it would come off, her mouth tasted like a sewer and the dryness around her tongue just added to the discomfort of having her hands tied behind her back and her feet securely fixed to the end of the iron bedstead. And as if that wasn't enough, she knew that if she wasn't able to relieve her full bladder soon, she would pee on the bed. *At least the bugger didn't gag me,* she thought as she tried to move herself into a better position. *I must have a pee.* She lay still and took stock of her situation. *It's no good screaming for help—no one's going to hear me. But Harry will be worried. Nat, too. But how will they look for me?* Maggie had to fight to control tears of self-pity.

The door to the room opened abruptly, and Maggie struggled to turn and face the new danger threatening her. It was Violet Larkfield, a gun in her hand.

"You're with us, I see," she said, kicking the door shut.

"What are you doing here?" Maggie rasped.

"Oh, didn't Cubby tell you? I'm in charge of hospitality around here."

"Nat will come looking for me, you know," Maggie said desperately.

"He doesn't even know you're missing. And even if he does decide to look for you, Cubby's ready to help with the search.

They'll never find you!"

"Nat will find my car," Maggie cried.

"Oh, your car's quite safe," Violet laughed, "tucked up in my garage." She turned to leave the room.

"Please, please untie me."

"Now why would I do that?"

"I've got to use the toilet."

Violet stood for a moment, deliberating. "Well... but if you try anything... roll over." Placing the gun on the table, Violet pushed Maggie over onto her side and slowly untied the rope holding her wrists. Picking up the gun again, she retreated to the door. "You can untie your feet at your leisure," she said, laughing maliciously. "Hope you make it before you wet yourself."

Maggie rubbed her wrists until the circulation came back. Painfully, she sat up and moved herself down to the bottom of the bed to where her feet were tied. Undoing the knots was another matter, and long before her feet were free, she was sure that dear Violet would have her wish and she would flood the bed. At last, still feeling dizzy, she staggered into the adjoining bathroom and crouched on the toilet. *Nat must know I'm missing,* she thought. But reality told her that he probably thought she'd stayed home because she was sick. Even if he called her home, Harry would never admit she wasn't there. And if he went to Violet's, the house would be empty and her Morris hidden in Violet's garage. "There's nothing for it," she said to herself with determination. "I've got to get out of this myself."

NAT WAITED IMPATIENTLY for Harry to open the door. "Come on, I know you're in there," he muttered through gritted teeth. Suddenly, the door jerked open, revealing a tight-lipped Harry and beside him a grim-faced young woman. "Mr. Spencer, I'm Nat South—"

"What have you done with my wife?"

"You'd better let me in," Nat answered, pushing past them. "We've got some talking to do."

"You haven't answered my question," Harry said, trailing behind him.

"Don't be a goddam idiot. Just tell me when you last saw her."

"Don't talk to my father like that."

Nat raised his eyebrows at the girl and then turned to Harry.

"This is my elder daughter, Barbara," Harry explained.

"And you," Barbara said spitefully, "must be this... detective or whatever you are that my mother has got herself mixed up with."

"Yes," Nat answered quietly, "your mother and I work together. Now, Mr. Spencer, when did you last see Maggie?"

"I saw *Margaret* last night."

"What time last night?" Nat asked, trying not to let his temper get the better of him.

"I don't know," Harry answered tartly.

"You don't know?"

"I think she was going out somewhere."

"Didn't she tell you where she was going?"

"No."

"Good God, man, was she in the habit of going out without telling you?"

"We'd had a bit of a dust-up," Harry mumbled, as he poured himself a Scotch and water.

"Weren't you concerned when she didn't come back?"

Harry's face flushed. "I wasn't aware that she hadn't come home," he said, knocking back the Scotch.

"You don't sleep in the same room?"

"I thought she had decided to sleep in the spare room."

"And you didn't check?"

"No. I just thought..."

"My father naturally thought she was with me," Barbara cut in.

"Yes," Harry said quickly. "I thought that's where she'd gone. Anyway, I'm sure she'll soon come to her senses."

"You called the police?"

"I don't intend to look like a fool when she turns up."

"Mr. Spencer," Nat said tersely, "has it occurred to you that Maggie may be in danger?"

"What danger could she possibly be in?"

Nat picked up the receiver of the phone and dialed. "Brian," he said when he had been connected, "I've a Mr. Spencer here whose wife's missing. He wants to talk to you about it." He held the phone out to Harry. "Sergeant Brian Todd of Missing Persons. Talk to him."

Harry's face blanched. "I told you I don't wish to bring the police into this."

Nat brought his face close to Harry's, "Talk to him, man," he said menacingly and thrust the instrument into Harry's reluctant hands.

"I don't see the necessity for calling you, but Mr. Southby insists."

"How long has she been missing, Mr. Spencer?" Todd asked.

"Since last night," Harry replied.

"It really depends on the circumstances, but we don't consider a person's missing till forty-eight hours have elapsed."

"Southby's sure something's happened to her."

"And you don't think so, Mr. Spencer? Put Nat back on."

"What's this all about?" Todd asked, when Nat picked up the phone.

"Maggie, that is, Mrs. Spencer, works for me."

"Yes?" Todd prompted.

"And we've been working on Ernie Bradshaw's murder."

"Farthing did mention you'd been poking your nose into one of his cases."

"I've a feeling she's followed a lead and got herself into some kind of trouble."

"Without telling you, Nat?" Todd asked. "I can't see a secretary going off on her own like that."

"For God's sake, Brian. Her husband hasn't seen her since last night, and she didn't turn up at the office this morning." Nat paused. "She would have phoned."

"You know there's not much we can do," Todd answered. "Unless you have proof of foul play, our hands are tied until the forty-eight hours are up."

"Wait a minute! I've thought of something," Nat said desperately. "Her car . . . it's missing too. Couldn't you put out an APB?"

"Use your head, Nat. Perhaps the lady doesn't want to be found. We'd look pretty foolish pulling her over."

"All I ask is that you keep a lookout for it."

"Okay, off the record, we'll keep an eye open. What's the licence number?

"What's the licence number of her car?" Nat said, turning to Harry.

"VBB 545," Harry answered.

CHAPTER THIRTEEN

As Nat drove back to his apartment, he mulled over the last telephone conversation he'd had with Maggie. She'd asked about Cubby. How long had he known him? And then that peculiar remark about cream in his coffee. He arrived home, parked his car in the alley and took the stairs up to his apartment. "Got to do something," he muttered as he headed for the kitchen, struggling out of his jacket. Five minutes later, a mug of instant coffee in hand, he walked back into the living room, sat down at his desk and reached for a yellow pad and pencil. "What the hell was she onto? And what in hell have I done with my cigarettes?" Back in the kitchen, he searched his jacket pockets until he found a crumpled pack of Camels, lit one and inhaled deeply before returning to his desk. "Now I can write."

Blue Plate Café, he wrote, then reached for his telephone directory. "I should have listened when she was telling me about the place. Just didn't think it important... Ah, here we are. North Vancouver. Why all the way over there, I wonder?" *Violet's*. "But I warned her not to go back there alone." *Collins*. "I'll call him in the morning." He flicked ash into his empty coffee mug. *Cubby*. "She seems interested in him for some reason." *Daughters*. "Not Barbara for sure. Maybe the other one." *Cops*. "No." *Hospital*. "I can check them out right now." He reached for the phone.

Two hours later, he collapsed onto his bed. He had exhausted all the hospitals, rechecked the morgue, called the Blue Plate Café and got no answer, then called Sawasky at home to find that his friend had gone to Toronto on business for a week.

MAGGIE OPENED THE WINDOW and leaned out. Faraway islands, wreathed in a light evening mist, seemed to float on a sea of gold while the last rays of the sun bathed the distant mountains in tones of apricot and deep pink. She leaned out as far as she could, looking for a means of escape, but discovered that even if she was able to climb out, there was nowhere to go but down to probable death. The house had been built high on a rocky bluff, and even if she could have found a way to climb down, there would be no soft cushion of earth to fall on. Just endless rocks and trees all the way down a hundred feet or more to the water. Looking down made her head spin, and she staggered back to the bed, where she lay down and closed her eyes. *Where in hell am I? I've got to get away.* The terror of Cuthbertson returning forced her eyes open again. *He'll be back.* There had to be another way out of this mess. Somehow she would have to elude Violet.

As if on cue, Violet opened the door. "Just checking," she said. She threw a sleeping bag into the room. "Here, you'll need this." She was pointing the automatic at Maggie.

"How long are you going to keep me here?"

"If it was up to me, I'd finish you off right now. You're nothing but trouble."

"They'll be out there searching for me."

"And a lot of good that'll do them," Violet said, backing out the door. "You're on a private island, my girl. No neighbours and, in case you're thinking of escaping, no boat."

When she was alone again, Maggie gave in to fear. *My God! What am I going to do? If only I could think straight.* She forced herself to her feet, headed for the bathroom and splashed cold water over her face. *There are no clues to connect me to this island. Nat thinks Cubby's his friend, and if it's true that he's gone to help Nat with the search, he'll consider Cubby even more of a friend.* She dried her face and walked back to the window again.

The sky had darkened and stars were beginning to come out, and in the distance she could see twinkling lights on one of the small neighbouring islands. She turned to go back into the room when it hit her. Lights! So Violet was lying. There were neighbours. A long way off, maybe, but there were people out there. *Of course, they may be friends of Cuthbertson. But even if they're not, how can I possibly get to them without a boat?* Exhausted and still suffering from the effect of the drug Cuthbertson had injected, Maggie crawled into the sleeping bag. "I must stay awake and think this out," she muttered as her eyes closed.

THE WATER GLINTED in the early morning sunshine and gently lapped against the moored boats in the yacht basin. Nat, groggy from lack of sleep, walked down the ramp to Cubby's cruiser. To his surprise, he found him lounging in a canvas chair on the afterdeck, smoking a cigarette, his face tilted toward the sun.

"You seen Collins around?" Nat asked.

Cuthbertson opened one eye. "Not for a couple of days. Come aboard. Sorry I can't offer you coffee."

"I'll buy you one over at the clubhouse," Nat said. He had used the last of his bottled instant during the night and left home this morning caffeine-less. He peered down the companionway into the cabin. "All the comforts, I see," he said, then, noting the dishevelled bunks, asked, "You living on board?"

"No. I didn't get in from fishing until the wee hours, so I decided to sleep here." He leaned over and closed the small door. "Let's get that coffee."

"Maggie's disappeared," Nat said as they walked side by side. "She hasn't been seen since Sunday night."

"Oh? Probably had a fight with her husband and walked out on him. Women are like that."

"Maggie's not like that."

"I guess you've tried all the usual channels."

"Yep. No dice."

"Stop worrying." He held the door open for Nat. "She'll turn up." Later, as he reached for his third creamer, Cuthbertson asked, "So why are you looking for Collins?"

"I think he's up to no good," Nat answered. "The police are taking a close look at his brother-in-law, too."

"You mean Larry?"

"There's a definite connection between him and the Cosgrove girl—the one they found dead with *Seagull*'s life jacket on. They think he's in deep with some kinda scam."

"A scam?" Cuthbertson asked quietly.

"Yeah. Missing girls. I'm worried Maggie has stumbled onto something," Nat said, trying to catch the waitress' eye. "More coffee, Cubby?"

"No." Cuthbertson stood up abruptly. "Sorry, I've got to run. I forgot I've got an important meeting this morning."

"That's okay," Nat answered. "I'm going over to Collins' berth again to see if he's turned up there."

"So you think Collins is in this thing with Larry?"

"Yeah. Maggie's convinced that both he and Violet Larkfield are mixed up in it."

"Violet Larkfield...? Ah, yes. Larry's aunt." He placed his hand on Nat's shoulder. "Look Nat, call me if I can be of any help. I mean it. Anytime."

That must be one hell of an important meeting, Nat thought as he watched Cubby climb into his green Mercedes and wheel out of the parking lot with tires squealing. In fact, Cubby, with murder in his heart, was heading for a showdown with Larry.

The canvas cover on Collins' boat was battened down, and pieces of paper and other debris that had been whipped by the wind clung to the canvas and the windscreen. Nat whistled. "This is one fast baby," he said, noting the boat's sleek lines and its powerful Johnson. He unbuttoned one side of the canvas cover and pushed it back so that he could see into both the forward and aft cockpits. Everything was clean and neatly stowed, and it was obvious that the boat hadn't been used for days. He buttoned the cover down again and headed for McNab's little cubbyhole of an office, but the only sign of the feisty Scotsman was a note pinned to the door: "Back Wednesday." Nat glanced at his watch. Maggie had scheduled a new client for eleven, and he realized with a sinking feeling that she wouldn't be there to greet the man and keep him happy until he turned up. He headed for his car.

It was well after one o'clock before he walked into the Blue Plate Café and sat down amongst the blue cloths, curtains and paper napkins. He ordered a club sandwich and fries and hoped that it would come on a regular white plate, having discovered a sudden aversion to blue.

"Do you remember a lady coming in here last week and asking some questions about missing girls?" he asked the young waitress as she filled his cup.

The girl shook her head. "Nah."

"Could you ask one of the other waitresses for me?"

"It *is* lunchtime, you know," she answered in an aggrieved voice. Nat opened his wallet and placed a two-dollar bill on the table. The girl bent down and neatly palmed it. "I'll ask."

Nat stared at the grey banana pudding that came with the lunch and decided against it. He was lighting his second cigarette when an elderly waitress stopped by his table.

"You wanna know about those missing girls, too?" she said.

"My assistant came here asking about them last week. Do you remember her? Short brown hair, blue eyes . . ."

The waitress nodded. "Yeah. A very nice lady."

"Can you remember what questions she asked?"

The woman thought for a moment. "She was mostly interested in these two guys I was telling her about. The guys that the girls came here with."

"What made you remember them?"

"The girls were so young." She checked to see if the boss was watching her. "Not that it means anything these days."

"Can you remember what the men looked like?"

"I'm not very good with describing people. Just what they eat, and like I told your girlfriend, funny habits."

"Habits? What kind of habits?"

"Well, like I told her, the older one of them uses a lot of these things." She pointed to the dish of coffee creamers on the table. "In his coffee, see. Then he builds them up, you know, like this." She leaned over him, picked up several of the containers and piled them on top of each other. "Sort of like building castles. Makes a hell of a mess."

Remembering the cream Cubby had spilt on the table that morning, Nat nodded in commiseration. "How old was this guy?"

"Oh, around about your age, I guess," she answered. "But he's a real snappy dresser, now I come to think of it," she added, eyeing Nat's crumpled suit.

"Any idea when you last saw either of them?"

"Not for a long time."

"How long?"

"Must've been over a month or more."

Nat stood. "I'll probably be back," he said.

The waitress started to walk away, then turned back. "You're not the police, are you?" she asked nervously. "I don't want no trouble."

"No." Nat got one of his grubby cards out of his wallet and thrust it at her, along with a five-dollar bill. "Look, if either of them comes in again, will you call me immediately?"

As he drove back over the Lions Gate Bridge, heading for his office, Nat went over his conversation with the waitress again and again. "What the hell did you find out from that waitress, Maggie, that I didn't find out?" As he neared the office block, he suddenly changed his mind and headed for Sawasky's precinct to see if there was anything new. But when he got there, he suddenly remembered that his friend was still in Toronto, and Nat was forced to talk to Farthing instead. He told him that Maggie was missing, but Farthing seemed uninterested. He checked in at the morgue again, then just to make sure, he canvassed all the hospitals once more. Nothing. He phoned Harry just in case she'd returned, and got his snotty daughter on the line instead. "No, Mr. Southby, she hasn't returned." Click. He phoned Violet Larkfield. Still no answer.

IT WAS AFTERNOON when Maggie finally woke. She lay trying to orient herself, then the horror of Cuthbertson coming back to kill her came flooding back. She wriggled out of the sleeping bag and ran to the window. *Damn! I can't see the dock from here.* Thank God her head was clearer, but she was almost faint from hunger. And there, just inside the door, was a tray with a bowl of canned stew and a cup of coffee. Both were cold, but she ate, relishing each mouthful as she surveyed her prison. One bed. One chair. Slatted blinds covering both the bedroom and bathroom windows. A single towel in the bathroom. And that seemed to be that. The only nice thing about the whole room was a huge confetti braided rug that covered most of the floor. *I think you're in a helluva fix, Maggie old girl. Not even a bedsheet to tear up.* She peered down at the rocks again and shuddered. "There's got to be another way out of here!"

Impossible schemes ran through her mind. Like screaming for help until Violet came up, then hitting her over the head with something—except there was no "something" to hit her with. Or getting Violet up to the room and pretending she was sick—except that would mean appealing to Violet's better nature, and she didn't think she had one . . . except with cats. She could try flashing the light off and on in the hopes that someone on one of the islands would come and investigate—except there was only a small bedside lamp with a very short cord. In the end, she had to face the fact that there was only one avenue of escape—the window.

The sky had clouded over and, shivering, she closed the window, walked to the door and pressed her ear against it. She couldn't hear a thing. *He can't be back yet. He would've come up. But why hasn't he come back?* She paced back toward the bed, tripped over the edge of the braided rug and landed with a thump. *Damn!* She turned to sit against the bed to survey the damage to her knees. "Just bruised," she muttered, and started to get up, then stopped. She stared at the offending rug and, for the first time in days, a little smile lit her face.

BY SEVEN NAT WAS HOME, making himself a stale cheese sandwich. He popped a beer and sank down in his leather armchair, but his mind kept coming back to Maggie's obsession with Violet and Collins. For the next hour, he sat stolidly in front of his television, staring at *Ozzie and Harriet* and then at some God-awful quiz show, without absorbing a thing. At last he turned it off and stood up, brushed the crumbs from his jacket and put on his shoes. "Violet, I'm coming to see you!"

The sky was heavily overcast and the house in complete darkness. Like Maggie before him, Nat parked a few houses away before walking back. At the front door, he leaned on the buzzer for several minutes before deciding the woman definitely was not home. He felt in his pocket for his penlight, and following its thin light, walked around to the rear of the house. By the time he located the stone steps up to the back door, he wished that he had returned to his car for his emergency lantern. He was just congratulating himself on reaching the door without a misstep, when out of the blackness a small body ran between his legs. He gave a yell, overbalanced, and his flashlight went flying. As he sat on the bottom step, the cat settled into his lap and began to knead his leg. "Well, if Violet's in, she sure as hell heard that," he muttered, pushing the cat away. He grabbed the flashlight, which was sending its thin beam skyward, held his breath and waited. But all was quiet. He staggered back up the steps and peered through the glass. He couldn't see a thing.

The cat sat hopefully by the door while he searched in vain under the sisal mat for a key. He flicked the light over a huge terracotta pot serving as an umbrella stand, then carefully tipped it up and felt underneath it. Still no key! "Maybe it's inside the pot," he said to the cat, who was watching him with keen interest. Removing a couple of tattered umbrellas, he thrust his hand down inside the pot. "Presto!" He pushed the key he'd found into the keyhole and gave a gentle turn. As the door opened, the cat slipped through the gap to disappear into the blackness. The overpowering feline odour made his stomach curl as he too slipped into the kitchen. He felt along the wall for the switch, and in the sudden light saw a door leading into a fair-sized dining room and another opening into a square hall with a staircase and the entrance to the living room. The house had a quiet, unoccupied feel about it, but taking no chances, he switched the kitchen light off before moving toward the living room. As Maggie had told him, there was the cat perch, and on each small platform sat a cat, its eyes reflected in the beam of the flashlight. But when one huge Siamese stood up, growled, hissed and then arched its back as if to spring, Nat ducked quickly out, closing the door behind him. Upstairs he opened the doors of three bedrooms before he came to what seemed to be Violet's. Risking the light again, he saw clothes strewn over the double bed, dresser drawers lying open and a suitcase discarded by the closet door. "Now I wonder where she went in such a hurry?"

A car's lights turning into the driveway and sweeping over the room caused him a moment's panic, but he resisted the urge to dive for the light switch. As the new arrival entered the house, Nat slipped out of the room to listen from the head of the stairs.

"Come on, you little buggers." It was Collins' voice. "Come and get it."

Nat risked looking over the banister to see Collins, like a modern pied piper, leading the pack of cats from the living room to the kitchen to be fed. He could hear him talking to them while he fed them and cleaned out litter boxes. Then, just as Nat turned to slip back into the bedroom, he felt something brush against his leg. Looking down, he saw a black cat twisting and purring in ecstasy.

"Get lost," Nat whispered, giving the cat a kick. But the animal was not about to leave its new-found friend, and standing on its hind legs, the cat stretched up and dug its claws lovingly into Nat's leg. *Holy shit!* He bent down, unhooked the cat's claws and gave it another shove, but it just purred louder and entwined itself through his legs. Stepping backward to get away from its caresses, he bumped into a small hall table. "Hell!" he breathed. Quickly, he moved back into Violet's room and made for the clothes closet, hotly pursued by the cat. They reached it in a dead heat just as Collins bounded up the stairs to investigate.

"Is one of you little buggers up here?" Collins said as he came into the room. "What the hell? She's left the damned light on!"

The cat gave a plaintive meow, and Nat pushed himself further into the closet until he was smothering in Violet's fur coat. Collins opened the closet door and the cat walked out. "How the hell did you get in there?" he said. He scooped up the cat, turned out the light, closed the door and went back down the stairs.

After Collins had left the house, Nat quickly disentangled himself from Violet's furry embrace, picked up his discarded flashlight and ran down the stairs. *She must have asked Collins to look after the cats,* he thought as he let himself out of the house. *And if I'm quick, I can follow him and see if he's the one that's holding Maggie.* As he ran down the street for his car, he saw a flash of silver as Collins drove past.

Nat started the engine and pushed the old Chevy into gear just in time to see Collins make a right onto Fourth Avenue. "He's heading downtown," he muttered. He soon realized that it was going to be very difficult to keep Collins in view and not be seen. He had to content himself with staying well back as he drove through the light Monday night traffic, hoping the occasional silver glint he saw reflected from the overhead street lamps would lead the way. Nat knew that Collins had a factory on Johnston Street on Granville Island, but when Collins turned onto the Granville Street Bridge, it became apparent that it was not his destination. His route took them instead onto Georgia and then through Stanley Park and over the Lions Gate Bridge before heading for Marine Drive in West Vancouver. Nat overshot Collins' next sharp left turn toward the water onto Bellevue Avenue, and by the time he had made a quick U-turn to follow, he was just in time to see that the Jaguar had been parked in a RESIDENTS ONLY car park adjacent to the luxury, eight-storyed apartment building that Collins was entering. Nat parked his car further up the street and walked back to the apartment building. There was a securely locked, strong glass door leading into a sumptuous lobby, and according to the residence list outside the door, Collins and his wife lived on the second floor. Although there was a faint possibility that Maggie was being held prisoner in their apartment, he somehow doubted it, because the man would hardly have left her there to go and see to his aunt's cats. He spent a few more minutes looking for Violet's or Maggie's cars outside the building, then climbed wearily into his own again. *That was one helluva wild goose chase*, he thought, as he headed back to Violet's place. *There has to be a reason why she left in such a hurry. And I still think the reason has to be Maggie.*

It was close to midnight when he arrived once again at the house at Seventh and Larch, and he spent the next hour scouring it for clues, even searching the desk in the living room amid the menacing cats, but finding nothing incriminating, he let himself out the back door, locked it behind him, and walked dejectedly to his parked car. "So," he said, reaching for his notebook, "she's not with Collins. She's not at Violet's. So where the hell is she?" He pushed the key into the ignition and then paused. *I wonder if Violet took her car?*

EXCEPT FOR A LITTLE FRAYING on the edge closest to the door, the rug was in good condition. The nail scissors she kept in her handbag would have cut the stitches that held the braids together in a matter of fifteen minutes, but she had left her bag in her car when she decided to become a super sleuth. *Think, Maggie, think. There must be something sharp somewhere in this prison.* Heart pounding, she crept to the door to listen once again for Cuthbertson's voice. Then, lying flat on her stomach, she peered under the bed. Nothing! The medicine cabinet in the bathroom was completely bare. Not even a safety pin. Apart from the one towel on the rack, a bar of soap and a toilet paper roll, that seemed to be it.

She knelt on the floor and looked under the old-fashioned, claw-footed bathtub. Thick grunge covered the floor under it, but in the far corner she could see a small silver handle sticking out of the filth. *A man's safety razor!* She stretched her right arm as far as it would go—it was so close, but not close enough. She stood up to survey the room for something to extend her reach. Then, hot and frustrated, she leaned over the tub to pull up the plastic slatted blind and open the very small window. The blind came clattering down again. "Damn!" Climbing into the tub, she snapped it up again, holding it up while she opened the window. And then it came to her. "Of course," she said almost happily, "one of these lovely slats will do it."

She yanked the blind down, pulled one of the slats out, then, down on her stomach once again, she began scraping the razor toward her. The slat seemed to have a mind of its own, and as she pushed, it bent double and suddenly sprang back to edge the razor further into the grunge. Maggie lay flat for a moment. "Patience, patience," she said, gritting her teeth, but it was all she could do to remain calmly on her stomach when she knew that even now they could be on their way up to kill her.

She tried again. This time she slowed her movements and concentrated on keeping the slat as taut as possible. Gradually, it came toward her and the razor was in reaching distance. With a cry of triumph, she grabbed it and sat up. "Oh my God... Violet must have heard me!" She sat still and listened. But all was quiet. Taking her treasure into the bedroom, she sat on the floor and began sawing at the stitches binding the braids together, but the blade was dull and rusted, and each stitch took minutes of hacking.

It was dark by the time she managed to separate two complete rounds of braid and sever them from the rug. She went to the window and looked down. A radio was playing in another part of the house, and leaning further out of the window, she could see light streaming from one of the downstairs rooms. *Wonder if that's Violet's room?* The night was moonless now, so it was too dark for her to see the ground below and the awful distance she would fall.

Gathering up the braid, she was dangling it out of the window when she heard the dreaded footsteps. Violet was coming back for the tray. Maggie hauled in the braid, threw it into the open doorway of the bathroom, switched out the light and ran for the bed. It wasn't until she was wriggling down inside the sleeping bag that she remembered the razor. *Oh! No!* It lay right where she had left it on the edge of the rug. But it was too late. Violet was opening the door. Maggie, desperately trying to keep her breathing even, prayed that Violet wouldn't put on the light to look at her and decide to give her another hypodermic. *Please, please, don't let her see the razor.* She lay still while the woman bent over her.

"You're not fooling me, lady. I heard you running around, but it's not going to do you any good. Your time's about up!"

Maggie heard her start to walk toward the door, then stop. *Oh God. She's coming back!* But Violet continued to the door and left the room. Maggie willed herself to stay motionless until at last she heard Violet's footsteps going down the stairs.

Trying not to make the bed squeak, she climbed out of the sleeping bag, bent down and removed her shoes so she could move more quietly. *There's got to be something I can use for a weapon in case she comes back.* Even if she risked putting the light on, she knew that it was futile to look for anything in the bedroom. *I'd better pee before the great escape.* Feeling her way into the bathroom, she sat on the seat and leaned against the tank. The lid shifted a little, and automatically she reached around and pushed it back into position, but her hand paused there. "My weapon," she whispered. Carefully, she lifted the heavy porcelain lid, then carried it into the bedroom to place it upright beside the door to the hall.

Dragging the braid from the bathroom, she took it to the open window and dangled it down the side of the house again. The wind was rising now and in the blackness down below, she could hear the waves raging against the rocks. She waited until her eyes became accustomed to the dark, and when the moon made a brief appearance, she leaned out the window. Even in the dim light she could see that the braid would only reach halfway down the huge rock face below the house. She hauled it back up, then sat on the floor and desperately hacked at the rug until she had another twenty feet of braid, then tied it to the first section.

I'll need something light-coloured to show me where it ends. She felt for the little scarf she had knotted at the neck of her sweater. "Gone, dammit!" she muttered. *The towel will do the trick.* While she tore at the towel, her mind went to the next step of her escape. She would need something to tie the braid onto. The bed was the only thing heavy enough, but to be of any use, she would have to drag it nearer to the window. Carefully, she double-knotted the braid to one of the bed legs, then tied a piece of towel to the other end, and began tugging the bed toward the window.

Anxiety rising, she dangled the braid out of the window, then, leaning out to check on it, she froze. The light from the uncurtained downstairs window was flooding the area below, and before she could haul the rope higher, a sudden gust of wind blew the knotted towel against the glass. She held her breath, expecting Violet to come storming up the stairs, but nothing happened. Calm again, she decided that she was as ready as she'd ever be.

It was while she was reaching for her shoes to put them on again that she heard Violet's tread on the landing. *Oh, no! Not yet.* There was no time to haul in the rope or push the bed back.

Instead, she slipped behind the door, and picking up the tank lid, raised it as high as she could.

"What the hell's going on . . . ?"

Violet's enraged voice was suddenly cut off as the porcelain lid came crashing down on her head, and she sank to the floor without so much as a groan. Maggie knelt beside the woman and was relieved to discover that she was still breathing. Taking her by the legs, Maggie dragged her further into the room, then rushed over to the window and hauled in the braid. It took valuable minutes to tie Violet up and make a gag with a strip of the towelling, then she raced out of the room and down the stairs.

Wrenching the front door open, she ran out into the night and realized that it had started to rain. Cold reason made her stop. A jacket! Running back into the house, she pulled coats and sweaters off the pegs beside the door until she found a floater jacket. *Shoes! I left my shoes upstairs!* Fearing that Violet would come to, she stuck her feet into the hiking boots parked beside the front door. *Damn! They're too big.* It was then that she heard the sound she had feared—a boat engine. "Oh my God! He's coming."

Slithering on the loose stones in her oversized boots, she was halfway down the steep path to the water when she realized that the engine had stopped and the dock landing was bathed in light. Diving into the wet bushes beside the gravel path, she huddled there, praying that Cuthbertson hadn't heard her rapid, noisy descent. She couldn't control her body shaking, or the dry, rasping breaths that wracked her chest, and she clasped her hands over her mouth to stifle the sounds. It seemed an eternity before she heard his boots crunching on the gravel path as he climbed toward the house, and then, just as he approached the place where she was hiding, he suddenly stopped. *He's seen me.* But Cuthbertson was only stopping for breath, and after a few minutes, he continued plodding his way up. She eased her cramped legs and stood up.

"Violet!" Cuthbertson roared. "Why the hell's the front door open?"

Galvanized into action, Maggie slipped from her hiding place and started down the path again. But as she neared the dock, the lights went out and she was plunged into a velvety blackness. *Oh my God! Cuthbertson must have put them out from the house. That means he's likely to put them on again when he realizes that I'm gone.* Panicked, she pushed her way into the bushes to the left of the dock and found a rough trail that followed close to the water's edge. Salal and blackberry bushes lined the path, catching Maggie's hair and clothes as she hurried past in the darkness. The rain that had started as she left the house had settled into a steady drizzle, as she stumbled over slippery rocks and treacherous roots. The hiking boots were far too big for her, and the effort of tensing her feet to keep them on slowed her down.

The trail swung inland. The blackberries gave way to small fir trees and low bushes, and the path became steeper. She clambered up the incline by hanging onto roots, her feet skidding on the loose rocks and sending small stones clattering down the hill. Then, panting with exertion, she managed to haul herself up onto a flat ledge of rock, where she lay, too exhausted to go any further. Home—and even Harry—would be a welcome sight at the moment. She wondered if she'd ever see them again.

CARRYING HIS EMERGENCY LANTERN, Nat retraced his steps to the back of Violet Larkfield's house. This time, however, he carried on past the porch until the lantern's beam flicked over the rear of the garage. It was then that he realized there was also a small shed attached to its rear wall. He tried the door, but it was locked, and heavy drapes covered the small window. The back entrance to the garage was also locked, but that door had a window in it, and he felt around in the dark garden until he found a hefty stone. "Better not wake the neighbours," he muttered as he wrapped his raincoat around his find. Seconds later he had a hole big enough so that he could reach inside and unfasten the lock.

His light flicked over the small red Morris parked inside. He checked the licence plate. VBB 545. Maggie's car! The driver's door was unlocked, and slipping into the seat, he reached across to the glove compartment. Violet had left nothing to chance—even the car's registration was missing. He checked under and down the sides of the seats, leaned over and searched the back seat, and then thrust his hands down the side pockets. As he reached up to the sun visor, a slip of paper fluttered down onto his lap. He scanned it eagerly, but it was just a grocery list. "Damn!" he said. He was about to crumple the piece of paper but stopped. There was some faint writing on the back. He flattened the paper on his knee and focussed his light on it. *Coffee creamers*, it read. "That damn coffee cream again," he exclaimed, and hauling himself out of the little car, he thrust the paper into his pocket.

It took him longer to break into the little room at the back of the garage, because the window was smaller and the glass thicker. Frustrated, he slammed the stone so hard on the window that he was sure that all the neighbours would come running. Sinking into the shadows of the garage, he waited, but there were no shouts of alarm or flinging up of windows. Feeling safer, he pulled out enough of the glass so that his arm would go through. Once inside, he fished in his pocket for his not-too-clean handkerchief to wrap his bleeding knuckles, then, throwing caution to the wind, put on the electric light. There wasn't much to see. A small living–kitchen area and at the back an alcove with a single bed.

But on the floor beside the bed, contents spewed, lay Maggie's handbag. He would know it anywhere. She had bought it with the first paycheque he had handed her and had laughingly called it her *Independence Bag*. Frantically, he wrenched open the doors to the closet and the tiny bathroom, but there was nothing. *Where could they have taken her? It had to be they of course, because Violet couldn't have done it on her own. She would need help. Who? Collins? Somehow he didn't think so anymore.*

He had stuffed the contents back into the bag and started toward the open doorway when he noticed the muddy footprints on the linoleum floor. *It must have been raining when she was here.* He knelt on the floor to examine the prints. *These look like runners. And they're the right size for Maggie, but these larger ones are . . . deck shoes!*

A few minutes later he was sitting in his car, with the rain pelting on the roof. "Deck shoes," he muttered. *It has to be Larry! And if it is him, Maggie was taken somewhere in a boat.* He looked at his watch. "Bloody hell! It's nearly two o'clock! What am I doing just sitting here?" He slammed the car into gear and drove off.

He made it to the yacht club in less than half an hour and eased the car into the first empty parking spot. Only a half dozen cars and as many boat trailers were parked on the lot, so the field was narrowed considerably, but he had no idea what kind of car Violet drove.

Within fifteen minutes, he had examined every car and boat on the lot, flashing his light into interiors and looking under each vehicle and into every boat, without seeing anything that he could tie to Maggie's disappearance. Cubby's boat was not in its berth, he noted with regret. "I could have used his help right now," he muttered.

Returning to his car, he flashed the beam on the rear of each vehicle as he passed it. Then suddenly, he stopped! Hanging out of the trunk of a dark green Mercedes was the corner of a pale blue silk scarf. "It's Maggie's!" For the moment, he was frozen. "Oh my God, she can't be in there!" He banged frantically on the lid. "Maggie! Maggie!" Then, racing to his own car, he opened the trunk, and among the collection of junk, found the tire wrench. He pelted back to the Mercedes. "Hang on, Maggie! I'm coming." Frantically, he tried to pry the lid open, but Mercedes are built to thwart theft, and all he managed to do was badly scratch the paint. He leaned back on the car to catch his breath, then, with grim determination, walked to the front of the car and, with a mighty swing, smashed the passenger window. He paused for only a second to listen for someone raising the alarm before reaching for the hood lever to see if the owner, like so many other drivers, kept a spare key hidden there.

Luck was with him, at last. There, hidden behind the windshield washer container, was taped a shiny key. Yanking the key from the tape, he raced to the rear of the car and unlocked the trunk. Empty! He stood there, crushing Maggie's scarf against his face. "My God, Maggie, where has that bitch taken you?" He studied the car again, running his flashlight over it from front to back in the first streaks of dawn light. "Wait a minute. This isn't Violet's car. This is the car Cubby drove off in this morning!"

CHAPTER FOURTEEN

It was barely dawn when Maggie awoke with a start. Then the horror came flooding back to her. *I can't stay here.* It had stopped raining and in the increasing light, she could see the trail that she'd climbed in the dark. From the ledge of rock she was standing on, the path led upward more steeply through thick salal with tall firs and arbutus overhead. Looking downward, she caught a glimpse of the sea below. In the night it seemed that she had climbed for miles, and it came as a shock that she wasn't as far from the house as she had hoped. There were two boats at the dock now, and she thought she recognized one of them as the *Seagull*. "I *was* right about Collins." Then she saw a movement below on the path. *They're coming!* As she plunged into the salal, the voices of her pursuers wafted up to her in the still morning air.

The higher she climbed, the steeper the trail became. She pulled herself up using the roots and rocks lining the path, her breath rasping in her throat. *Oh, God help me!* she found herself praying over and over to a God she wasn't at all sure existed. She pulled herself over the rim of another rock ledge, and not realizing that she was out in the open, she paused momentarily to reconnoitre. There was a sharp crack and something splintered the boulder just to the right of her, sending shards of rock flying, one of them gashing her cheek. Instinctively, she let go of the root she was holding to touch the blood that was trickling down her face. The laugh from below made her frantically search for the root again and use it pull herself to the relative safety of the salal engulfing the next part of the path. Taking a quick look down through the brush, she saw that Cuthbertson and another man were already standing on the ledge where she had rested only fifty feet below her. Cuthbertson was holding something to his shoulder. *A rifle!* Hanging onto a strong root with her left hand, she reached over to a large rock imbedded in the earth and wrenched it free. It went scudding down through the underbrush, taking a shower of pebbles with it. The yell from below told her it had found its mark, but she knew that it wouldn't hold them up for long.

In sheer desperation, she found the strength to pull herself even higher up the slope, and glancing upward, she could see that the rough trail veered slightly to the left. She had to get there before Cuthbertson used his rifle again.

His sarcastic voice floated up to her. "There's nowhere to go, Maggie."

She hesitated for a split second before reaching for another rock. "Damn you!" The muttered words rasped out of her dry throat as her scratched and bleeding hands wrenched more rocks and gravel out of their holes. Her feet in the over-large boots searched for footing as she resumed the climb, and then the left boot started to slip off. Desperately, she clenched her foot to keep it on, but it was no use. The boot went sliding down the slope and she cringed as she heard the crow of laughter from the men below. Another crack of the rifle and the zing of the bullet hitting the ground just above her made her cry out in terror. Her feet went from under her and she found herself swinging in the air, hanging onto a large root by one hand. Reaching over to a boulder to steady herself, she scrabbled in the gravel to regain her footing. She didn't even try to stop the second boot joining its companion, but the sound of the two men laughing even harder just gave added impetus to her determination to escape. The muscles in her arms screamed in pain as she pulled herself up and around the curve in the path.

She lay on her stomach momentarily and drew in great gulps of air, but the sounds of the two men scrambling up behind her quickly got her to her feet. Sobbing, she clambered up the remaining boulders onto a narrow animal track and began to run. But although the going was easier, her bare feet marked every stick and stone, and she realized it would be much easier for her pursuers in their boots.

The track, weaving in and out of the towering salal, monster ferns and other straggling bushes, was almost tunnel-like, but every now and then she caught glimpses of blue sky and sunlight filtering down through the trees, and she realized that the path lay just below the ridge that formed the summit of the hill. Gasping and holding her side, she ran faster, but the tree roots caught her feet, and she lost time as she climbed over the broken branches that littered the path.

Thwack! The bullet ricocheted off a large fir tree. They were closing in on her now. *Oh, my God! Oh, my God!* In spite of her exhaustion, she picked up speed. It seemed that she had been on the track for hours, climbing over fallen logs, wading through streams and slipping down gullies. But after awhile there was no more shooting. They were probably so confident of getting her in the end that there was no need for them to hurry. They could save their ammunition to finish her off.

Suddenly, the trail divided. One path continued below the summit and the other, she could see, plunged downhill. Sliding downward on the loose gravel, she felt her feet going from under her and grabbed at the small trees and bushes that lined the path. When she hurtled out into the open, she found that she was on the edge of a sloping cliff. Where could she go? The voices of the two men quickly made up her mind for her, and she launched herself downward on her backside toward the sea crashing on the rocks below.

Dazed, bruised and bleeding, she came to rest on a small stretch of pebble beach. The incoming tide crashed over her legs, and Maggie, lying on her back, looked up at the watery sun peeping through the low scudding clouds. What was the use of running anymore? They would get her eventually. She had nowhere to go. She had nowhere to hide. All they had to do was shoot her where she lay.

"Damn you!" she cried. "I'd rather drown."

She rolled onto her bleeding knees and forced herself upright. Stumbling over the slippery green rocks showing so clearly through the icy water, she waded deeper and deeper until the rocks fell away beneath her and she started to swim.

NAT GAZED HELPLESSLY at Cubby's empty berth. "You did your best to tell me about the bastard, Maggie," he said out loud. "I was too dumb to see what you were getting at." The ghostly grey mist hanging over the deserted yard and the slight breeze that rocked the boats gently at their moorings gave the whole place a look of unreality. He shivered, turned on his heel and started up the ramp to his car. "Collins," he muttered. "That's who I need to talk to."

He parked in the first available RESERVED FOR RESIDENTS spot, bounded up the steps to the apartment building's entrance and leaned on Collins' buzzer. While he waited, he caught a glimpse of himself reflected in the polished brass mailboxes and saw an unshaven, hollow-eyed man looking back.

"Who the hell is it?" Phillip Collins' voice came over the intercom.

"Southby."

"It's damn near four in the morning!"

"Lemme in."

"Get lost!"

"It's important."

"Call in the morning."

"Look, Collins, it's about . . ." Nat realized that he was talking to a dead receiver. He leaned on the buzzer again.

Collins' irate voice answered. "Go away or I'll call the cops."

As Nat reached for the buzzer again, the entrance door opened and a bleary-eyed man carrying a lunch pail shuffled out into the chill morning. Nat grabbed the door before it swung closed and raced for the stairs. He took them two at a time to the second floor and hammered on Collins' door.

It opened suddenly and Collins, wearing only striped boxer shorts, stood glaring at him. "I warned you, Southby . . ."

"Let me in." Nat pushed past him into the foyer.

"What the hell's going on?" Collins still held the door open.

"Quiet!" a man shouted from the doorway of the adjoining apartment. "Some of us want to get some sleep."

"All right," Collins said in resignation, closing the door, "but it had better be good."

"Just tell me," Nat said, grabbing the other man's arm, "are you in on this scam with your wife's aunt or not?"

"Scam? What the hell are you talking about?"

"This baby racket. Smuggling. Whatever it is."

"Who is it, Phillip?" A blonde twenty years younger than Collins—her hair mussed, puffy face smudged with last night's makeup—appeared, clutching a pink satin robe around herself.

"Go back to bed, Steph," Phillip Collins snapped. "I'll deal with this." Then, turning to Nat, he said, "You'd better explain."

"Maggie Spencer is missing."

"Maggie Spencer?" Collins asked, mystified.

"And the Larkfield woman has something to do with it."

"Aunt Violet?" Stephanie Collins came further into the room. "She couldn't be."

"Your aunt is capable of anything," Collins said scathingly.

Nat turned to the woman. "Larry's your brother. Right?"

"So what?"

"There's at least three of them in this thing—Cuthbertson, your brother and your aunt—and Maggie stumbled onto it."

"Who the hell is Maggie?" Collins demanded.

"My secretary, that's who! And I need your help."

"What can I do? I don't know anything about it!" Collins answered in exasperation. "And what's all this got to do with you and your secretary?"

"We got called in to find Ernie Bradshaw's cat, then your boat got smashed up, and old Ernie was murdered..."

"But Larry explained about the boat, honey," Stephanie interjected, gazing anxiously at her husband.

"I bet he didn't explain that he was smuggling pregnant teenaged girls across the line with it," Nat answered her.

"Larry wouldn't do that..."

"Shut up, Steph! Let him get on with it."

As quickly as possible, Nat explained the situation. "And Maggie figured it out and that's why they took her," he ended up.

"My brother wouldn't be mixed up in anything like that." Stephanie Collins turned to her husband. "Tell him he's wrong, Phillip."

"Your brother's a rotten little bastard," Phillip Collins said to his wife. "I should've known he was up to something illegal."

"You've never liked him," Stephanie cried. "You think you're too good for my family."

"For Chrissake," Nat interrupted, "let's get on with it."

"You've got to believe me, Southby," Collins said. "I didn't know anything about this!"

"But you must know where the hell they could have taken her!"

"We don't even know this Maggie person," Stephanie said, shrugging.

"Where does Cuthbertson go when he's out fishing? Does he own a summer place? A cabin or something like that?"

"No," Stephanie answered quickly. "He doesn't have anything like that."

"Yes, he has, you little bitch!" Collins turned on his wife.

Stephanie's face paled. "No, I . . . I . . ."

"I know about your little . . . junket with Cuthbertson."

"But I . . ." Stephanie stammered.

"Going to visit my sister," Collins mimicked.

"For Chrissake," Nat snapped. "Stop bickering. Where is it?"

Stephanie crossed her arms over her chest and looked toward the window. "I don't remember."

Collins grabbed her arm and put his face close to hers. "Tell him where the place is, or I'll . . ." He let the sentence trail off.

"You're hurting me," Stephanie whimpered, trying to pull herself away.

"It can't be more than a few hours away," Nat interjected. "He was back here with his boat the morning after Maggie disappeared."

"Tell him, Steph," Collins said, pushing her toward Nat.

"It's on an island."

"Where? What's the name of the island?" Nat demanded.

"I don't remember," she sobbed. "He'll kill me."

"And I'm going to kill you if you don't tell him where it is,"

Collins said in a low voice. He turned to Nat. "I'll get a map from my desk."

"It's only a little island," she said, turning to Nat.

"Please try and remember where," he pleaded.

"We stopped at this place near there for groceries. Pender Harbour, I think it was called."

Collins returned with a survey map and spread it on the table. "Now, Steph," Collins said, grabbing his wife roughly by the arm, "point to where the island is."

"There's so many," she wailed.

"How long did it take you to get from Pender Harbour to the island?" Nat asked.

"I dunno. About twenty minutes, I suppose," she answered.

"Is it a small house? Big one? What?"

"It's big."

"Can you see it from the sea?" Nat asked in exasperation.

"There's lots of trees."

"Did *you* see it from the sea?"

"It was dark. He only turned the dock lights on after we landed," she answered sullenly.

"What are you going to do?" Collins asked, letting go of his wife's arm.

"Right now," Nat said, striding to the telephone, "I'm calling Mark Farthing. He's with the homicide squad."

"You can't bring the police into it," Stephanie Collins pleaded. "What about Larry and my aunt?"

Nat looked with loathing at Stephanie's tear-streaked face. "I think they deserve everything they get."

Nat had to hold the phone away from his head when Farthing heard his voice. "Now what?" he shouted.

"I know where she is."

"Who?"

"Maggie. If you listen, I'll fill you in."

"Make it fast."

"There isn't much time, Farthing. Please just listen . . ."

"You can use my boat," Collins offered. "I'll get changed and come with you."

THE HEAVY SWELLS OF the incoming tide and the weight of Maggie's clothing hampered her efforts to swim. The nylon floater jacket would have to come off. Treading water and inadvertently taking huge gulps of seawater, she struggled to get her arms out of the jacket and watched it drift away. Among the logs floating in the tide was a branched tree adorned with seagulls, and she swam to it and grabbed at a jutting branch. The gulls rose, shrieking at her intrusion, and Maggie, scared that they would alert her pursuers, plunged deep under the derelict tree and came up cautiously on the other side among its branches. Looking back toward the shore, she could see the two men standing on the cliff's edge, peering out to sea. Numb with the intense cold and choking on the salt water as she bobbed up and down on the waves, she watched them confer. Cuthbertson pointed down to the beach, and the other man—who she was now sure was Larry Longhurst—promptly slid down the steep slope and started to search along the narrow strip of beach. Her focus was on Longhurst when there was a sudden shout from Cuthbertson and she saw him point out to sea. *Oh my God!* The jacket. She watched him raise the rifle and fire.

Terrified, she submerged again, hanging onto a tree branch. She held her breath as long as she could, then, cautiously resurfacing, she glanced around. To the right of the cliff was a headland and beyond it a small cove. Keeping her head low and forcing herself to swim slowly, she began to push the rolling log toward the headland.

NAT PUT THE PHONE DOWN. "Farthing will be here in twenty minutes."

"Do you want my boat?" Collins asked.

"No. He says the Coast Guard just got their first Sikorsky helicopter and they're itching to use it. But he wants both of you along for the ride."

"No!" Stephanie cried. "Not me."

"We're both going," Collins said to his wife, pushing her toward the bedroom. "Get your clothes on."

Nat watched the two of them go down the hall, then, sinking into a leather armchair, he closed his eyes. The sharp ring of the phone on the table beside him had him on his feet in an instant. "Yeah," he barked into the instrument.

"Sarge says to be down on the street when he gets there. And bring your map."

As he replaced the receiver, Nat looked up to see Collins coming back into the room. "She's putting on her makeup," he said in disgust.

Nat zipped his jacket and the two of them started for the front door, neither of them noticing that the red extension light was glowing on the telephone. A few minutes later, Stephanie came down the hall. "Do I have to go, Phil?" she whined. "You know how I hate planes."

"You're going," he answered and held the door open for her.

"You're the only one who can identify the place," Nat said.

"Not from the air," she wailed.

"Come on, let's go," Nat ordered.

On the way to the Richmond airport, Farthing leaned over to Stephanie. "I'm counting on you to show us where this island is."

"I keep telling you guys it was dark when I was there."

"How long were you there? A few hours? Overnight?"

She gave a sideways glance at her husband, who was sitting

beside Nat. "Overnight," she mumbled.

"Then you did see the place the next morning!" Farthing said triumphantly.

"I . . . uh . . . I stayed in the cabin coming back. It was cold."

"You must have known something was going on between your brother and Cuthbertson," Farthing persisted.

"Why should I?" she answered quickly. "It was just me and Cubby there."

"How far did you say it was from this island to Pender?" he asked.

"I already told you. I don't remember."

Farthing leaned back in the seat. "I hope for your sake, Mrs. Collins, your memory returns once we're in the air."

It was six-thirty by the time they arrived at the airport. On the way, Farthing had been on the radio, making last minute arrangements for the helicopter and talking to the Coast Guard in Pender. The rotors were in motion when they pulled into the terminal. At any other time, Nat would have been thrilled at the prospect of his first flight in one of these remarkable new craft, but all he wanted now was for this monster to get off the deck. The bright yellow aircraft seemed immense as they climbed aboard through the five-foot sliding door into the main cabin. The pilot made a quick introduction to Sandman and Kepler, his two crewmen, who in a matter of minutes had Nat and the Collinses buckled into the fold-up seats that faced each other on either side of the long, wide body. Farthing took one of the front seats near the pilot, the map spread out over his knees.

Once airborne, Herb Sandman walked to the rear and lifted down one of the black wetsuits hanging there on pegs.

"What are you doing?" Nat shouted above the noise of the engines.

"There might not be a place to set down on the island. Got

to be ready to go in by sea," Herb shouted back.

"I'm coming," Nat said, unbuckling and jumping up from his seat.

"You done any diving?" Herb said, looking dubiously at Nat's rotund body.

"All the time," Nat lied. "Gimme a suit."

"I'll see if it's okay first," Herb said, and he staggered up the aisle to the front.

Nat could see both the pilot and Farthing vigorously shaking their heads, but not waiting for the outcome, he lifted down the largest wetsuit he could find and was already struggling out of his clothes when Herb returned.

"They said no," Herb said.

"I'm going. Now help me into this thing."

"But . . . but they said . . ."

"Listen, I'm going. It's my fault she's in this mess. I'm going with you, so just get that straight."

Sandman shrugged. "Okay. But it's going to be tight," he said. "Here, hold on." He reached into an overhead compartment, and taking down a can of oil, thrust it into Nat's hands. "You'd better douse yourself with this."

Glancing self-consciously at Stephanie and Phillip Collins, Nat stripped to his skin and began lathering himself with the oil.

Stephanie studiously ignored him by looking out of the window, but Phillip reached over, took the can of oil and rubbed it over Nat's back and legs, then helped to squeeze him into the suit. But even well lubricated, Nat didn't get suited up until they were nearing their destination. The zipper refused to go all the way.

Sandman glanced at his watch. "We should be over the area by now," he said as he unstrapped one of the inflatable lifeboats from the bulkhead. He dragged it to the sliding door and placed it next to the winch and sling, ready to be lowered.

Except for a few misty patches swirling around the islands and coastline, the weather had cleared. "Good Sunshine Coast weather," the pilot said to Farthing. "Sun, rain and fog."

The tightness of the wetsuit was restricting Nat's breathing, and as he stared down on the grey, choppy waters, he lowered the zip another couple of inches. "Please don't let us be too late," he muttered to himself.

RETCHING AND SHIVERING, Maggie pulled herself up slippery green rocks into the shallow water of the cove. High eroding tides and strong winter winds had created large hollows in the banks, which in turn had bared the gnarled tree roots of the scrub evergreens fighting for existence above. It was to one of these hollows that Maggie managed to drag her aching body, and she lay, wet and shaking with the cold, curled in a fetal position, to wait for her nightmare to end. Since the cove faced away from where the two men were searching, she knew that for the moment she was relatively safe. She closed her eyes.

"Poor Emily. Hold on, little cat. Harry will feed you." She scrubbed a hand over her face. "Sorry, Harry," she muttered and drifted into a fitful sleep.

The sensation of water lapping over her feet brought her suddenly awake. She tried to sit up and pull herself closer to the wall of the hollow, but she was too exhausted. Instinctively, she knew that she was suffering from hypothermia, but she lacked the means or will to do anything about it, and she let unconsciousness overtake her.

Unable to find her, the two men had given up the search along their stretch of beach and had made their way back to the house. "We'll take *Seagull* and check out that jacket," Cuthbertson said as they neared the dock. Steadying himself, he placed the rifle in the aft cockpit and then climbed in behind the wheel.

"What for?" Larry answered him. "She'll be drowned by now."

"Use your loaf, man," Cuthbertson said, looking with loathing at the younger man. "If that jacket's keeping her afloat, somebody else could find her."

"Yeah. See what ya mean," Larry said. He untied the bowline and climbed in after Cuthbertson. The powerful engines surged into life as Larry leaned over to untie the stern line.

"Now what does that bloody woman want?" Cuthbertson said irritably, watching Violet running down the path, waving her arms at them. "What's she saying?"

"Turn the goddam motor off," Larry yelled over the noise. "Just go up and find out what she wants."

Reluctantly, Larry climbed out of the boat and loped up the ramp to meet Violet. Cuthbertson watched the two talking and then Larry ran back to the boat.

"They're on to us, man!"

"Who? What are you talking about?"

"My sister was on the phone. It's that fucking dick."

"You mean Southby?"

"Yeah. He's got you figured."

"He can't do a thing from there!"

"He's on his way. With the cops."

"Bloody hell," Cuthbertson said. He slammed the boat into gear, and it rocketed from the dock with the bow high in the air, cutting through the waves and leaving a creamy wake behind. Larry, who was about to leap into the boat, fell into the water instead. Violet came screaming down the path, and rushing to the edge of the dock, threw herself down and extended her hand to her nephew. Choking on the salt water, Larry heaved himself up onto the dock, where he lay gasping for breath.

MAGGIE, IN HER semi-conscious state, was unaware that she had rolled out of the scant shelter of the hollow and that the sea, now at full spate, was lapping over her violently shivering body.

FARTHING STARED DOWN at the small islands that dotted the Strait. "How can we be sure which one it is?" he asked over the intercom.

The pilot pointed to two fairly large islands apart from the others. "There's only houses on those two," he said. "I know. I fish in these parts, and I've checked them all out."

Farthing nodded. Carrying the map, he walked back to where Stephanie Collins was huddled against the bulkhead. "Recognize either of these?" he asked, pointing down to the islands.

"No," she answered, not bothering to look.

"I want you to have a good look. The pilot will go down closer for you." Giving Farthing a venomous look, she turned sullenly away from him to gaze out of the window. "Do you recognize anything?" Farthing said again in exasperation.

She shrugged. "No."

Stifling the urge to shake her, he worked his way back to his seat. The pilot, having circled the two islands, now headed east into the sun that had risen just high enough to crest the coastal mountains, casting golden patches across the peaks. The men, binoculars pressed against the glass, found the light so dazzling that they were momentarily blinded. Completing his turn, the pilot headed west again, and Nat rubbed his eyes and took another look through his glasses.

"Hey! Farthing, look!" he yelled. "There's a boat going like a bat-out-of-hell."

Up front, Farthing indicated to the pilot to descend, and he leaned out of the window to have a closer look. "There's only one man in it. Could be anyone."

Suddenly, Collins jumped from his seat and pushed past Nat. "That's my boat!" he yelled. "That shitty little bastard has taken *Seagull* again!" Collins was apoplectic. "I'll kill that little . . ."

Nat leaned over Farthing's shoulder. "It's that son of a bitch Cuthbertson at the wheel!"

"You sure?"

"But where's Maggie?" Nat made to open the sliding door. "If he's harmed her . . ."

Herb grabbed him. "Let's do this right," he said calmly, making a circling signal to the pilot.

Cuthbertson, glancing up at the helicopter, made a bid to outrun it, but then, realizing that it was still gaining on him, he cut the engine back and reached for his rifle as the helicopter began to circle over him again. He saw the two men in the open door and recognized Nat. "You meddling son of a bitch," he muttered as he raised the gun.

Nat and Herb, standing ready in the open door, ducked as they saw Cuthbertson raise the gun to his shoulder. "We've got to stop him," Nat shouted.

Herb nodded. "We will," he said grimly. Then he made a down motion to the pilot.

Cuthbertson's shot went wild, and dropping the rifle to the deck, he reached for the controls again and pushed the craft to its limit, wheeling hard to the left, but the boat was no match for the copter's manoeuvrability. He looked up just in time to see Herb kicking a huge cargo net overboard. "What the hell . . . !" He was knocked off his feet as the net fell over him and then became entangled in the motor. It spluttered, and then kicked back with a loud bang. The boat reared up, then subsided in its own swirling wash.

"My boat," Collins wailed. "What have you done to my boat?"

"It can be fixed," Herb said grimly. "Anyway, that'll keep him quiet until the Coast Guard picks him up," he said. "Now let's go and find your Maggie." He gave a thumbs-up signal to the pilot, who immediately flew in the direction of the boat's wake toward the largest of the occupied islands.

Farthing, who was on the radio giving the Coast Guard directions for picking Cuthbertson up, was startled when Collins suddenly yelled, "There's the little bugger. There, on that dock!"

Nat and Herb immediately trained their binoculars to where he was pointing. "Violet's there, too," Nat yelled back. "But where's Maggie?"

Larry, looking up to see the helicopter coming toward them, jumped up in panic and ran toward Cuthbertson's boat.

"Wait for me!" Violet screamed at him as he jumped aboard.

"They're taking the other boat," yelled Nat. "We've got to stop them."

But as they neared the dock, they saw Larry jump out of the boat again, carrying something. He turned to face the chopper. "Look out," Herb yelled. "He's got a gun!" The bullet zinged close to the open doorway, making everyone in the helicopter duck.

As the pilot veered away, Nat could see Violet still standing on the dock, screaming at Larry as he headed up a narrow trail leading into the bush. "We've got to catch him," Nat shouted. "Can you get us closer?"

"Too many trees," the pilot yelled back. He swung the craft back over the water and then began to fly along the shore in the direction that Larry had taken.

Farthing reached for the radio. "I'll call for extra help."

"But what about Maggie?" Nat was beside himself. "We've got to find her!"

"Calm down, Southby," Farthing yelled at him. "The police cutter will be here soon and they can search the house. We've got to see where that little punk has gone."

"Open beaches ahead," the pilot called out as he hugged the

rocky edge of the island. "Watch for him coming out into the open."

Nat grabbed Herb's arm. "Look," he yelled. "There's someone over there."

Herb reached forward and indicated to the pilot to go down lower.

"Is it Larry?" Farthing cried.

"It's someone lying on the beach." Nat leaned out of the open door. "Farthing! I think it's Maggie."

"I can't get any closer," the pilot yelled. "Herb, you'll have to jump."

"Too many rocks," Herb answered. "Take me out further and I'll jump with the life raft." He beckoned Nat to help.

Moments later, the life raft landed with a splash, with Herb jumping after it into the choppy grey sea, quickly followed by Nat. It seemed an eternity before he stopped descending into the cold black water, and he thought his lungs would burst. Then, to his relief, he began to rise toward the light. Spluttering and choking on the salt water, he broke surface, only to waste precious minutes orienting himself in the direction of the beach.

Herb had already reached the life raft, rolled himself over the side into it and unfastened the oars from its side. He paddled over to where Nat was choking, spluttering and attempting to swim toward the shore. Herb extended his hand.

"There's no way I can climb into that thing," Nat said, shivering with the intense cold that had seeped through the opening of the suit. "You get to Maggie."

"Hang on to the raft," Herb called to Nat. "I'll row."

Heavy swells made the going painfully slow, and although Nat had shown bravado in donning the wetsuit and jumping into the waves, it had been many moons since he had been for a swim in a pool, let alone the sea. As he laboured toward the beach, he regretted the extra weight he'd put on since he left the force. He even regretted his cherished cigar smoking.

As they neared the beach, Herb rolled out of the raft beside Nat so that together they could haul it carefully over the hidden rocks. But the huge breakers that crashed onto the shore created strong undercurrents that sucked their feet from beneath them and made them slip and slide on the slimy green stones. Eventually, dragging the raft behind them, the two men, bruised and gasping for breath, crawled to where Maggie lay. "Maggie!" Nat cried as he knelt down beside her. "Is she dead?" he asked Herb. "My God, is she dead?"

Herb rested his head on her chest. "No, she's still alive. Come on, we've got to get her out of the water." Gently, they lifted and carried her higher up the beach.

"She's so cold," Nat said, gathering her to him.

"She needs warmth," Herb replied. "Get her wet clothes off." And he ran back to the raft for the emergency blanket. After rolling her into the blanket, Nat held her as close to him as possible and tried to impart some warmth from his own shivering body.

"Hang on, Maggie," he murmured to her. "Help's on the way. You're going to be all right."

"They're coming," Herb said, pointing out to sea.

Through the light mist they saw a police cutter speeding toward them, and in the distance, the sound of rotors heralded the return of the helicopter. As the cutter pulled close into the shore, an officer jumped from the deck and waded toward them through the breakers. "Have you seen Longhurst?" he demanded as he stumbled up the stony beach.

"Forget him," Herb ordered. "Just get this woman on board so we can transfer her to the helicopter. There's not much time."

Corporal Ritchie quickly knelt down beside Maggie and felt for a pulse.

"Blankets," he yelled to his partner. "On the double." Then he turned back to Nat. "She's in a bad way," he confirmed as he wrapped the extra blankets around her. "Kappa, you radioed the chopper yet?" he yelled to the man who was manning the boat.

"They're ready to lower the stretcher in about two minutes," Kappa called back. "Get her into the boat."

Nat insisted on helping to carry Maggie over the stones and into the waiting police boat and hovered over her as they moved out into open water. He watched in fear from the deck as the stretcher was lowered and she was quickly fastened into it and hauled to safety. "Do you think she'll make it?" he asked Herb anxiously as the helicopter flew off.

"I honestly don't know, Nat," Herb replied.

"You both need some warm clothing," said Corporal Ritchie. "Kappa, get them some dry gear."

As difficult as it had been getting into that tight wetsuit, Nat found it ten times worse trying to take it off. Eventually, as they neared Cuthbertson's dock, and with some help from Kappa, he was finally dressed in some jeans (tight and short in the leg), a T-shirt and sweatshirt (overly large) and runners that actually fit. He was ready to join in the hunt for Larry.

"We'd prefer you to wait on the dock," Ritchie said as they clambered out of the launch. "He's got a gun."

"I'm coming," Nat answered.

Ritchie shrugged. "Okay. But I warn you, keep behind me." He turned to Kappa. "You and Herb go up to the house after the woman." He led the way onto the trail.

Climbing up the rocky trail behind Ritchie, his feet slipping on the loose stones, Nat wondered how Maggie had managed to get down to the beach. *She must have come this way*, he thought. *But how could she have done it alone?* He realized what an awful ordeal she had gone through and knew that he was at least partly responsible, because he hadn't listened to what she'd been trying to tell him. They took a breather on a large ledge and looked back to where they could see the dock. Ritchie flicked on his walkie-talkie and spoke to Kappa. "They've picked up the Larkfield woman," he said, slipping the thing back into its case. "They're searching the house now."

"Why didn't Larry take Cuthbertson's boat?" Nat asked. "They could've got away."

"No ignition key," Ritchie said, laughing grimly. "Come on, let's get going."

"There've been several people on this trail," Nat commented as he reached up to grab a rope-like root. He pointed to the holes where stones had come loose and now lay scattered on the ledge. "And look at all the broken roots and branches."

"I wonder what these hiking boots are doing here?" Richie said, picking one up. "By the look of this terrain, you need 'em on."

Nat's mind slipped back to the image of Maggie lying on the beach with bloodstained feet. "Let's get on with it and find that little bastard," he said.

LARRY HAD REACHED THE FORK in the path. He had heard the coming and going of the helicopter and police boat while he had been running along the trail and felt quite confident that they would be too busy chasing after Cuthbertson and Violet to bother about him. Somewhere on the north end of the island was the cabin that Cuthbertson had told him about. He would hole up there until everything had died down.

NAT WAS FINDING IT TOUGH going to keep up with the younger, fitter man, and when he eventually reached the flat trail, Ritchie was well ahead of him. The pain in his side made him slow down to a walking pace. He noted the broken branches and recently trodden plants on the narrow animal track and wondered how far Larry had got since he took flight. *After all*, he thought, *the island can't be that big. Where could he possibly hide?* He came to an abrupt stop. The trail had suddenly divided and in his preoccupation he, hadn't seen which way Ritchie had gone. He decided on the upper one and broke into a run again. After about ten minutes, he realized that the muddy path was getting much narrower and even disappeared every now and again as it ran through dense salal, salmonberry bushes and ferns. He began to wonder if he had made a mistake and should turn back to where the path had divided. Then, rounding a bend, he saw a huge tree trunk lying across the path. Panting and sweating with exertion, he braced his hands on it to give himself a breather before retracing his steps. His hands touched mud. There were muddy footprints and skinned bark leading over the log. One set! Larry had come this way! Hanging onto the broken branches, he heaved himself up and over, and with renewed determination, regained the trail again.

The path led down a gentle slope, and as Nat pushed his way through the brush, he heard the sound of breakers crashing on the rocks in the distance. Sunlight and occasional patches of blue sky filtered through the thinning trees ahead, telling him that he would soon come out into the open. He forced himself to slow down and to tread as quietly as possible.

The old wooden shack nestled against a wall of rock came as a complete surprise. Its broken windows were draped with wild honeysuckle, an old shake roof was covered with moss, and a rusty stove pipe stuck out of one end of it. The wooden door was partly open. Cautiously, Nat moved toward it.

"Stay right where you are."

Nat whirled. Longhurst was standing about fifteen feet away, beside a lean-to covering a pile of firewood. There was a revolver in his hand and it was pointed at Nat.

"Don't be stupid, Larry," Nat said, taking a few paces toward him. "The cops'll be here soon."

"Back off." The hand holding the gun was shaking. "You can't fool me, old man."

"Hand over the gun, Larry." Nat took another step forward. "They've picked up Cuthbertson."

"Don't come any closer."

"They're onto you, Larry."

"They can't prove anything." Longhurst waved the gun at Nat. "Get into the shack. Go on!"

"They've also picked up your aunt," Nat said quietly, taking a few more steps. "She'll spill everything."

"Shut up! Shut up!" Longhurst screamed. "Get into the fucking shed."

Nat took another step closer and Longhurst's gun hand began to waver. With a yell, Nat sprang forward and lunged for the .38, sending the younger man crashing to the ground. But Longhurst was up on his feet immediately, giving Nat a smashing blow in the face. With a roar of pain, Nat lowered his head and rammed it into the other man's stomach, sending him and the gun flying. They fell to the ground, rolling and smashing at each other with their fists as each tried to gain control. Nat saw the gun just feet away and tried to roll toward it, but his tired body was no match for the younger man's. Larry smashed his fist into Nat's face, grabbed the weapon, and with a sudden twist was astride him, pinning him to the ground.

"Now what, old man?" Longhurst said, grinning, pointing the gun downward. Gathering all his strength, Nat tried to push Larry off and make another grab for the gun. The sound of the report as the bullet went through his shoulder nearly shattered Nat's eardrums. He fell back, dazed, and looked up into Larry's cold eyes as he lifted the gun once more and pointed it at Nat's head.

The pain of the bullet wound in his shoulder flooded over him in waves as he twisted under Larry's weight, trying to push him off, so it took awhile for Nat to realize that the next shot he heard was sending Larry reeling backwards instead of sending *him* to the next world.

"Bloody amateurs," he heard Ritchie say as he passed out.

CHAPTER FIFTEEN

Farthing, after leaving Maggie at the hospital and arranging transport for Collins and his wife, had returned by seaplane to pick up his prisoners and take Nat back to the city for treatment. And now, hours later, his arm in a sling and his face covered with cuts and bruises, Nat emerged from the Lions Gate Hospital's emergency room, only to come face to face with a raging Harry.

"Is she okay?" Nat demanded. "Have you seen her?"

"No thanks to you, she's still alive," Harry replied curtly.

"I'm truly sorry," Nat said, sinking into a chair.

"Sorry? Sorry isn't good enough," Harry said, standing over Nat. "If anything happens to her, I'll . . . I'll . . . sue you."

Nat patted the chair beside him. "Sit down, Harry. We'll wait together."

"You get away from me, you . . . you . . ." He turned away from Nat in disgust. "Don't you ever, ever contact my wife again."

The recovery room door opened and a white-coated doctor came out. "Nat Spencer?" he enquired. Both Nat and Harry stood up.

"My name is Harry Spencer," Harry said primly. "And I'm Margaret's husband. How is she?"

"Lucky," the doctor said. "She'll be okay."

"Can I see her now?" Harry asked, walking toward the door.

"Yes, but she keeps asking for someone called Nat. Do you know who she means?"

"No," Harry said angrily. "I'll see my wife now." The doctor looked puzzled, but he nodded and led the way inside.

Nat smiled weakly at the doctor's news, and walking back to his chair, sat down to wait. But the hours went by slowly. Sawasky, back from Toronto, turned up at the hospital and found a totally exhausted Nat asleep across three chairs. Taking matters into his own hands, he persuaded him to go home to bed. "I'll let you know when you can see her," Sawasky promised as he delivered Nat to his apartment. "Get yourself a stiff drink and sleep."

Early the next morning, nursing a thumping headache, Nat called the hospital to learn that Maggie's condition was "satisfactory." But still no visitors permitted except immediate family. Taking a cup of coffee to the telephone, he dialed Farthing's number. "What's happened?" he demanded when he was eventually connected.

"Ah . . . Southby," Farthing said in an unusually quiet voice. "I need to see you." He paused. "Say eleven this morning?"

"But what about Maggie? When can I see her?"

"I'll see you around eleven," Farthing replied. The line went dead, leaving Nat, frustrated and aching, glaring at the instrument.

PROMPTLY AT ELEVEN, Nat presented himself at the precinct, where he was shown into his old office and left to wait. *What does the son of a bitch want?* he wondered as he gazed around the room. Farthing had made a few changes since Nat had occupied the room. There were three certificates for athletic awards hanging on the wall behind the desk—Nat had never been one for overdoing exercise—a couple of framed photos showing Farthing with members of the police hockey team receiving a huge cup, a factitious smile on his face, and on the desk, a picture of a very pretty woman and a couple of kids in a silver frame. Nat shifted uncomfortably in his seat and wished the man would hurry up and get there.

The door opened and Farthing stepped in. "Sorry to keep you waiting, Southby," he said, going behind the desk and sitting down.

"What's going on, Farthing?" Nat demanded.

"Considering the part you played in the affair," the man intoned pompously, "I'm willing to bring you up-to-date on some of the circumstances, but then I have another matter to discuss with you. Which to my mind is far more important."

"Can you please make it quick," Nat answered shortly. "My arm is killing me."

"I will tell you about Cuthbertson and Longhurst first," Farthing went on in his ponderous way. "They're both out of hospital and in police custody. Cuthbertson sustained a broken collarbone when the net hit him, and the bullet from Ritchie's gun only winged Longhurst. You've got Ritchie to thank for saving your life, you know." Farthing paused for breath. "Constable Kappa arrested Violet when they found her hiding in the house. In spite of us finding the room where she held Mrs. Spencer, she denies being a part of it. Says it was all Cuthbertson. He, of course, immediately started screaming for his lawyer." He paused for breath. "That satisfy you?"

"Got anything from them?"

"Not yet."

"Have you spoken to Maggie yet?"

"The hospital says we can see her today, but . . ."

"I want to be there."

"Her husband's given strict orders that you're not to be allowed in."

"That stuffed . . ."

"That's all I can tell you."

"But I must see her."

"My hands are tied," Farthing said. "Her husband has the say until she's well enough to tell us what she wants."

"But . . ."

"Let it go, Southby. If she wants to see you, she'll ask."

Nat stood up. "Nothing's going to stop me from going there," he said grimly.

"Sit down, Southby," Farthing ordered. "There's this other business."

"For God's sake," Nat answered. "What other business?"

"The little matter of you taking payoffs just like your old boss Mulligan." Farthing smiled thinly. "I've got proof, you know."

"What the hell are you talking about, Farthing?" Nat towered over the other man. "Proof? What d'ya mean, proof? Proof of what? I never in my life took a bribe. Are you nuts?"

Farthing reached down and retrieved the folder from the bottom drawer. "This proof," he said. "You didn't make a very good job of cleaning out your desk. You left this behind." He opened the folder and took out the half sheet of paper. "I'll read it to you, just to refresh your memory—*I, N.M. Southby, accept the sum of three hundred dollars per month as settlement, and in return agree to make no further demands.* As you can see," he concluded, "it was signed July 1952. That would be around the time you were working closely with Mulligan, wasn't it?" With a smirk, he pushed the note under Nat's face. What he wasn't prepared for was Nat's reaction. Instead of being defeated, the man was actually laughing. In fact, he had to sit down and hold onto his aching ribs. "What are you laughing at, Southby? This is serious."

Nat wiped the tears from his eyes. "So that's what's been bugging you all this time, you jackass!" he said, gasping for air. "You know, if I wasn't in so much pain, Farthing, I'd cheerfully smash your stupid face." He shifted uncomfortably. "That document you've been so carefully hoarding was a draft of the monthly payment agreement with my ex-wife, Nancy Southby." He looked witheringly at Farthing. "Although it's none of your damn business, it was included in the final divorce settlement, notarized, and made legal by a judge." Painfully, he pulled himself up. "I'm leaving."

NAT AWOKE THE FOLLOWING DAY to brilliant sunshine. He rolled onto his back, stretched his one good arm above his head and planned his day. Call the hospital, breakfast in his usual café, a walk in Stanley Park and then to the office. It was time he got back to work. Dressing was still a painful business. The bruises had turned into various shades of yellow and purple, but flexing his good arm, he decided he was going to live. As he reached for the phone, it rang.

"Why haven't you been in to see me?" Maggie demanded.

"Maggie!"

"I've been waiting and . . . I just couldn't believe Harry."

"What do you mean?"

"That you wouldn't be coming in to see me."

"That son of a . . ." Nat took a deep breath to control the anger. "Maggie, I'll be straight over."

Propped up in bed, a pale, very weak Maggie greeted him with, "I'm sorry to have been so much trouble."

Laying the crumpled cone of flowers he had hastily bought from the local grocer on the bed, he took her hand in his, and asked, "Sorry? What the hell for? I'm the one who's sorry for getting you into this."

"Harry told me it was all because I meddled that the police had to get a rescue helicopter and . . . and . . ." Her voice trailed off.

"Meddled! Listen, Maggie my girl," Nat replied firmly, "if it hadn't been for your meddling, Cuthbertson and his lot would still be free."

"It was so terrible, Nat." Tears started to run down her face.

"It's over now," Nat said briskly, patting her hand. He wasn't very good at dealing with tears. "Now," he said, quickly changing the subject, "how did you cotton on to Cuthbertson?"

She gave a shaky laugh. "I kept telling you, Nat, the cream containers."

"Ah, yes. The cream. What about them?"

"Oh, Nat," she said, laughing. "He built castles with them. The waitress in the café told me about them."

"Of course," Nat said, as he recalled the mess Cubby had left when they'd had coffee together.

"Now," Maggie asked, "What's the whole story?"

"The trio's in custody. And Farthing's putting it all together. We'll know the rest in a few days." Nat bent over and kissed her awkwardly on the forehead. "Get better quickly, Maggie," he said brusquely.

"I'll be out in a few days."

He looked down at her, the old smile creasing his face. "Then we'll beard Farthing together." And with a wave of his hand, he slipped through the door.

"I HOPE YOU REALIZE what a worrying time you've put me through, Margaret," Harry said.

Maggie, sitting in her favourite chair and stroking the ecstatic, purring Emily, looked up in surprise.

"Yes," Harry continued. "The senior partner came in to see me. He was particularly put out."

"Alfred Crumbly? He was worried about me?"

"Not you, Margaret. The publicity."

"The publicity? I don't understand."

"Well," he said patronizingly, "the firm has a reputation to protect. But it should all blow over now that you're out of it." He reached for his drink and took a sip. "Glad to see you've come to your senses."

"What are you talking about, Harry?"

"Well, as old Crumbly mentioned—lots of women go through a difficult time at your age."

"My age?"

"You know," he said with an embarrassed cough, "the change of life thing. That's probably what sent you off the rails."

"But weren't you worried about me?"

"It goes without saying that the girls and I were very upset to see you in the hospital."

"Thanks, Harry," she said dryly.

"Yes," he continued, "but as Mother said, you've had your fling and now you can settle back to being a proper wife again. And you'll soon forget all about this . . . this . . ." His voice trailed off.

A feeling of intense exhaustion and sadness rushed over her. She leaned back in her chair and let the tears trickle unheeded down her face.

"You'd better go to bed, Margaret," Harry said briskly, picking up his book. "The doctor told me you will need lots of rest."

"FEEL UP TO SEEING Farthing today?" Nat asked when he called.

"You don't know how glad I am to hear your voice."

"Well, you've had a week to recover, and Farthing would like to see the two of us this afternoon. Two-thirty. You strong enough?"

"Of course I am."

"Good. You're beginning to sound like your old self again."

"Meet you at the precinct?"

"Come to the office and we'll take my car."

"Two o'clock?" Maggie said.

"Fine."

Replacing the phone, she bent down and swooped up a surprised Emily, burying her face in the cat's fur. "Oh, Emily, if it hadn't been for you, my life would still be so tame and uninteresting." *Now, what shall I wear?*

It was five after two when Maggie parked her Morris, which the police had returned to Harry during her hospitalization, outside the office building. Her boss was already on the sidewalk waiting for her. "I thought you weren't coming," he said. Maggie smiled as she climbed into his car.

A subdued Farthing gave a curt nod to Nat, and after shaking hands with Maggie, indicated the two visitor's chairs across from him. "Glad to see you've recovered, Mrs. Spencer. That was a bad affair."

Maggie drew her chair closer to the desk. "Can you tell us the whole story now? Were we right about the girls? Where did Cuthbertson fit in? And . . ."

Farthing put up a hand. "We're still putting things together. And whatever I say to the two of you today stays in this room. Do you understand?"

Both Maggie and Nat nodded. "We both agree to that," Nat answered, wishing the man would get on with it.

"As far as we can see, Larry and Violet got into the baby racket accidentally."

"Accidentally?" Maggie interrupted. "How . . . ?"

"If you wait, Mrs. Spencer, I'll explain," Farthing said. "Apparently, in his last year of high school, some girl told Larry that she was pregnant. God knows why she told him."

"Perhaps he was the father," Maggie suggested.

Farthing shrugged. "The girl in question was from a good Catholic family, so abortion was out."

"Where did Cuthbertson fit in?"

"A bit of a coincidence, I think," Farthing said, reaching for a cigarette. They waited while he lit up and finished coughing. "You see, Larry often crewed for Cuthbertson—we've since found out that they had a nice little drug-running business going between the States and the Gulf Islands."

"So Larry turned to him for help with the girl," Maggie said.

"Yes. Cuthbertson made the necessary arrangements, and before the girl showed too much, whisked her down to Washington."

"How did Violet get involved?" Nat asked, looking longingly at Farthing's cigarette.

"They needed a holding place, and Violet was willing to oblige—for a price."

"What happened to the girl?" Maggie asked.

"She was one of the lucky ones. They managed to slip her down to Seattle in Cuthbertson's boat. Arrangements were made for her to stay in a small private hospital until the baby was due, and when the time came, the woman who was buying the baby stayed there with her."

"I see," Maggie said slowly. "The girl leaves and the new mother takes the baby home."

"Yes. The birth certificate was made out in the woman's name and the girl, minus baby, returned home. All very neat."

"And her parents didn't suspect anything?" Nat asked.

"Apparently not. They were just so pleased to see the girl back." Farthing leaned forward and stubbed out the cigarette in the overflowing ashtray. "I guess they figured she'd just run away."

"How do you know about her?" Nat asked. "Was she listed as missing?"

"Her name came up quite a long time ago, when we started to pull all the files for missing girls that might fit into Larry's little racket."

"But you knew she'd returned?" Maggie said.

"Yes. Finally tracked her down. Very reluctant to talk at first. She's married now and doesn't want her husband or parents to know. But when I explained about the other girls, she agreed to talk."

"So the racket grew from that."

"Apparently. Cuthbertson and his US lawyer friend could see they were onto a good thing. We're talking tens of thousands of dollars here, you know. And between them they soon had a lucrative business going. Larry made the contacts in the different high schools and introduced them to Cuthbertson. But from the onset, they were very choosy."

"Choosy?" Maggie asked. "What's choosy about being pregnant?"

"The girls had to come from good middle-class homes—to impress the clients, no doubt—and they were not to be prostitutes, so they could rule out venereal diseases. And before Cuthbertson would agree to help them, they had to go through a thorough medical examination."

"He must know a cooperative doctor?" Maggie asked.

"But how do you know all this?" Nat asked.

"Cuthbertson ran out on Larry, so Larry spilled his guts to get even."

"But what happened to all the other girls?" Maggie asked. "According to your files, most of them are still missing."

"We've had a bit of luck there." He shifted in his seat. "Last week one of the girls escaped and managed to get to a telephone and call for help. The Seattle police have located the farm where the girls were held and have made several arrests. It'll take awhile to find all of them and their babies," Farthing added. "But we'll be working closely with the Seattle authorities."

"So Cuthbertson was cleaning up on these kids' misery?" Nat said.

"Yes," Farthing answered. "But we think that he and his crew got too greedy. Why give the girls a cut if they didn't have to? Also, they got worried that their money-making scheme would blow up in their faces if any of girls blabbed or had second thoughts about giving up their babies."

"So they kept the girls in the States," Nat said.

"Yes. As far as we can make out, the girls would be systematically drugged until they had a dependency and then put on the streets in Texas and Florida," Farthing replied. There was a silence in the room, and he added, "Maybe we'll be able to find some of them before it's too late."

"I hope Amy Holland is found in time," Maggie said quietly.

"We'll have a damn good try."

"But what about Ernie? Where did he fit into the picture?" she asked.

"Old Bradshaw?" Farthing stood to open the door for them. "We're not sure if he does fit in. Forensics are still at the Larkfield house looking for evidence that he was killed there." He paused for a moment. "But I think he must have stumbled onto their little scheme while searching for that cat of his—like his daughter said."

"Emily," Maggie said, tucking her purse under her arm.

"I beg your pardon?" Farthing asked, puzzled.

"His cat's name is Emily. And she's mine now," she said with a happy smile.

"Eh ... Southby," Farthing's voice faltered. "About that other affair ... Can we just ... uh, forget it?" He held out his hand.

Ignoring the hand, Nat followed Maggie out of the room.

"What other affair?" Maggie asked when they reached their car.

"I'll fill you in about that later," he answered, helping her in the passenger seat. They were both very quiet with their own thoughts as they drove toward the office.

"They murdered him, you know," she said as they got out of the car.

"Old Ernie? Yes, I'm sure they did." Nat opened the street door to the office building. "You coming up?"

Maggie hesitated for a moment and then followed him up the stairs.

The familiar dry office smell hit her as they walked into the room. Nat threw his hat in the direction of the coat tree, and as usual, missed.

Maggie ignored it. "I'm leaving Harry," she said quietly.

Nat's heart gave a thump. "I'm glad," he said.

Deliberately, she turned away and sat behind her battered desk. "Can I come back to work?" she asked.

He smiled. "You weren't thinking of leaving me to struggle here on my own, were you?" He walked over to the window to look down at the busy street. "Well, if you're leaving Harry, where are you going to live?"

"I don't know as yet, Nat. But I've decided to keep the cat, and for the sake of Emily, I have to find a small house or at least a basement apartment with a small garden."

"Great." Nat retrieved his hat from the floor. "We're both professional detectives. Come on, let's start looking."

DON'T MISS MAGGIE SPENCER'S NEXT ADVENTURE,
AS SHE PUTS HER SKILLS TO THE TEST IN THE CARIBOO

From *In the Shadow of Death*...

BY THE TIME the train had reached the coastal mountains after stopping at the small stations of Squamish, Whistler and Pemberton, Maggie thought that the scenery couldn't possibly get any better. She peered out of the dusty window of the three-coach train, awestruck by the beauty of the mountains, their snow and glacier peaks glinting in the morning sunshine. Then the scene changed to sheer tranquility as the track ran beside Duffy Lake, where the fir forest and mountains were reflected perfectly in the still water. Before reaching Lillooet, the train made a couple of stops to let passengers off. Most of them were met, and she watched as they threw their bags into battered pickup trucks or old cars. Once, the train even stopped to let a passenger off in front of his home. She watched the man throw his bag over the fence before hopping over it himself, then turn and give a cheery wave to the train's engineer, who gave an answering toot of the whistle before continuing down the track. But the area was so remote, the roads that ran beside the tracks so narrow and dusty, that she wondered how people could possibly live in such isolation.

✦ ✦ ✦

MAGGIE AND THE HORSE eyed each other warily. "Ever ridden before?" a voice said behind her. She turned to find a heavy-set man in his mid-fifties. He was dressed in jeans, western boots, red-checked shirt and the biggest Stetson she had ever seen. *This must be Hendrix.*

Kate made a perfunctory introduction, then hurried off to attend to her own mount.

"Not for quite awhile," Maggie answered, trying not to stare at his hat. "My sister has a riding stable in Norfolk, but I haven't been back there in awhile." She put out a tentative hand to stroke Angel's nose.

"Then you never used a western saddle?" He pointed to a mounting block. "Here, climb up."

Maggie was terrified that she would make a complete fool of herself and go flying right over the horse and land on the ground. But to her surprise, she found herself astride the animal. Hendrix adjusted the stirrups. "Okay," he said, "let's see what you can do." Swinging himself onto a huge chestnut mare, he leaned toward Angel and took the leading reins in his hand as they headed out of the enclosure and onto a well-marked trail. After her initial nervousness, Maggie soon found herself adjusting to the horse's gait, and she even managed to take an occasional glance at the open range as they plodded toward the distant hills.

Hendrix broke the silence. "You a friend of Kate's?"

"No. I rent a basement suite from her sister in Vancouver." Her gaze wandered up ahead to where Kate, looking very much at home on her horse, was chatting to the young ranch hand keeping pace beside her on his grey mare. "Kate looks as if she's doing okay."

"Yep."

"She's worried about her husband."

"Huh!" he snorted.

"You don't think she has cause to worry? He's been away for nearly two weeks now."

"Used to go away all the time before she come along." He leaned over and handed the reins to her. "Try riding on your own."

"If you're sure she won't charge off with me clinging to her neck."

"Just do what I showed you," he added. "Head for those hills up there."

"That seems an awfully long way."

"You'll make it," he answered in his terse manner. "You seem like a natural. You'll be sore when you get back."

"Kate and Al are coming back," Maggie said, hoping Hendrix would decide they'd gone far enough.

"Al's got chores to do."

"See you back at the house, Maggie," Kate called as they trotted past.

Maggie waved and then urged her horse to go a little faster to catch up to Hendrix. As they neared the base of the hills, he reined in his horse and looked up at a flock of birds wheeling in the sky. "What's the matter?"

"They're over the Black Adder Ravine," he replied thoughtfully. "Stay here while I take a look-see."

"No. I'll come, too," she answered, not wanting to be left alone.

"Probably a cow fallen into the ravine. We'll ride aways, then dismount when it gets too steep. You go ahead of me."

The higher they climbed, the steeper the ravine fell away on their left side, and Maggie was glad that Angel was very sure-footed on the loose gravel of the narrow road. She made an effort not to look down. After awhile, she stopped and let Hendrix catch up. "I think I'd better get down," she told him.

Hendrix nodded and steadied Angel while Maggie slid down

the animal's flank. "We'll leave 'em tethered here." He dismounted, took the reins of the two horses and fastened them to one of the saplings that lined the cliff side of the road, and they began plodding upward. Getting as close to the edge as she dared, Maggie craned her neck to get a better look at the top of the craggy mountain that towered over them.

"This road is literally cut out of the side of the mountain," she said in wonder. "Where does it lead?"

"An old mine. Hasn't been worked for at least fifty years, to my knowledge." For another five minutes, he led the way up the road, then suddenly stopped and pointed down into the ravine. "Christ! There's a Jeep down there."

Maggie stopped beside him. The Jeep was upside down, and a man's body lay on the rocks beside it. She grabbed Hendrix's arm. "We've got to get down there."

"No. We'll go back to the ranch for help. Come on." He turned and ran down the road to where they'd left the horses. "Come on." Maggie followed and when they reached the horses, he cupped his hand and helped her onto Angel

"You go on ahead," she said. "I'll be fine."

"You sure?" And when Maggie nodded, he jumped onto his own horse and raced back down the track, and was soon a cloud of dust in the distance.

IF YOU LIKED MARGARET SPENCER, CHECK OUT THESE OTHER TOUCHWOOD MYSTERIES

From Ron Chudley...

A gripping story of one man's search for his son, *Stolen* reveals how our intuition can propel us to answers that others may never have found. John's son disappears during an overnight stay in the Fraser Canyon, and though a body is never recovered, the authorities label the case a drowning, after finding the boy's teddy bear at the edge of the river. Convinced his son has been stolen, John embarks on a perilous search that strains his wits, and demands the blind faith found only in a parent *in extremis*.

"Chudley's third and best mystery novel grabs you by the throat and doesn't let go."—*The Globe and Mail*

ISBN-13: 978-1-894898-59-1 • ISBN-10: 1-894898-59-1 • PB $12.95

Also by Ron Chudley:

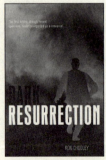

Dark Ressurection
ISBN-13: 978-1-894898-48-5
ISBN-10: 1-894898-46-6
PB $12.95

Old Bones
ISBN-13: 978-1-895898-33-1
ISBN-10: 1-894898-33-8
PB $12.95

From Stanley Evans...

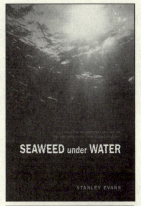

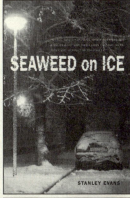

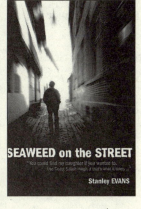

Silas Seaweed is the street-smart and savvy Coast Salish Native detective in Stanley Evans' successful mystery series. Suspenseful and compelling, Silas' cases often take him from the city's highest and lowest classes, to find the buried crimes that link them.

"The writing is wonderful native storytelling. Characters are richly drawn ... I enjoyed this so much that I'm looking for the others in the series."
—*The Hamilton Spectator*

Water ✦ ISBN-13 978-894898-57-7
ISBN-101-894898-57-5 ✦ PB $12.95

Ice ✦ ISBN-13: 978-1-894898-51-5
ISBN-10: 1-894898-51-6 ✦ PB $12.95

Street ✦ ISBN-13: 978-1-894898-34-8
ISBN-10: 1-894898-34-6 ✦ PB $12.95

GWENDOLYN SOUTHIN was born in Essex, England and launched her career after moving to the Sunshine Coast of Canada. She co-founded The Festival of the Written Arts and the region's writer-in-residence program. She co-edited *The Great Canadian Cookbook* with Betty Keller and her short stories and articles have appeared in *Maturity, Pioneer News* and *Sparks from the Forge*. She is at work on more Margaret Spencer adventures, and lives in Sechelt, British Columbia.